# Stay-At-Home Detective

# Stay-At-Home Detective

By

Michael Gray

**Cataloguing in-Publication Data**

Gray, Michael 1986-
Stay-At-Home Detective.
Summary: Ned Gray solves a murder mystery, after unexpectedly becoming a stay-at-home parent to his three-month-old daughter McKenzie.
1. Mystery—Fiction. 2. Humorous Stories. 3. Cozy Mystery. I. Title


Produced by Michael Gray. All rights reserved.
Published by Amazon's Kindle Direct Publishing (KDP).

ISBN-13: 978-173-0764844

ISBN-10: 17-30764-843

First printing November 3, 2018.

*To my wife, Katie*
*Sorry I don't clean up the diapers more often*

# Chapter 1

I swear, you take one day off of work so your wife can retire, and you find yourself changing diapers for the next four years. Before you know it, you're accused of murder, and your entire life is turned upside-down!

At least, that's what happened to me.

My name is Ned Gray. I like to think I'm a normal guy. I've got a wife and kid, I work at an accounting firm, and in my spare time, I do video reviews for the *Harvey Brothers* book series.

Okay, maybe that last one isn't so normal, but it's a fun little side job. I know those books are made for kids, and they can be a little cheesy sometimes, but I like them anyway. I reviewed a couple of them on a whim back when I was in college, and things just sort of took off from there. Now I'm proud to say I'm the #1 reviewer of *Harvey Brothers* books!

Also, the only reviewer of Harvey Brothers books.

Getting back to my Weirdest Day Ever, it started with me, asleep in bed with my wife, as usual. I was violently woken up, when I was kicked in the side, twice. Then I got smacked in the ribs.

I rolled over to see why Brittany was trying to kill me in my sleep, and ended up getting a face full of baby diaper. The baby flailed her legs and kicked me again.

"I think McKenzie is awake," I said.

My wife grunted and turned her head to the side.

"And I think you're not," I added.

"Aaaaa," said McKenzie. She pawed at my wife's shoulder, while I stretched and got out of bed. I picked up my pillow and laid it down sideways. That way, it would serve as a barrier to prevent McKenzie from rolling off the bed by accident.

McKenzie watched me intently as I did this, then rolled over and tried to eat the pillow. Typical baby move.

I went to the bathroom and got changed. By the time I got back, my wife was sitting up and holding McKenzie.

"Good morning," I said.

"Morning," she replied. "Did you sleep okay?"

"I did, until our little kickboxer woke me up. You excited for your big day?"

"I wouldn't call it *my big day*, but yeah, I guess I'm ready." Brittany works at an insurance company as a claims adjuster. I think her job is way more interesting than mine—I just play around with numbers all day and hope they add up correctly—but she says it's not as interesting as it sounds. It's mostly filling out paperwork.

The company gave her three months of maternity leave when McKenzie was born, and those three months were up today. We had been hoping to find cheap daycare in the meantime, but no such luck. Brittany would have to quit her job to become a full-time, stay-at-home parent. I had already arranged to take the morning off so I could watch McKenzie while Brittany handed in her resignation.

Brittany sighed and shook her head.

"Is something wrong?" I asked.

"I don't know," she said. "I feel terrible about the whole thing. It feels like I'm cheating the company, you know?"

"You told them that you would probably quit after maternity leave was over."

"Yes, but I still feel like a scumbag. Like, 'Hey! I know you just paid me for three months, even though I did absolutely nothing for you! Now I'm quitting and taking my severance, so you can pay me even *more* for doing nothing!' "

"Hey, being a full-time mom is important. Isn't that right, McKenzie?" The baby opened and closed her mouth like she was trying to talk, but didn't know how to form the words. "She agrees with me."

Brittany half-chuckled. "You can go to her room and change her. I'm taking a shower this morning."

I took McKenzie upstairs to her changing table. There is basically no *way* my wife and I would put up with having diapers in our bedroom.

Once she was changed, McKenzie stared at me. "Hi, McKenzie. It's gonna be just you and me today."

McKenzie started crying. Not the best way to start the day.

It didn't take a genius to realize she was hungry. I took her back downstairs so Brittany could feed her, but it was too late. My wife had already started her shower. McKenzie started screaming louder.

"It's okay, it's okay," I said. "Mommy will be out soon. Then she can feed you."

McKenzie sometimes has screaming fits when it's bedtime, so I knew what to do. I walked around and rocked her back and forth. That worked for a few minutes, until she got bored and remembered she was hungry. Then the screaming resumed.

"Shhhh! Shhhh! Would you like a song? Song?"

She screamed louder. I started singing while walking her around, and the screams subsided for a while. Again, this trick only worked for a few minutes. Daddy songs are nice, but they're not as important as full bellies.

It seemed like an eternity before Brittany was finished. By that time, McKenzie had stopped screaming, and she was whimpering loudly. I looked at my wife, and I immediately forgot what I was going to say.

It was the first time in months that I had seen her in work clothes, and I have to admit that I stared at her a little bit. She looked really nice with a crisp shirt and creased pants. Her black hair was pulled back into a tight ponytail, showing off her large purple earrings. She almost never wears earrings anymore, because the baby likes to pull on them.

3

Brittany looked at me for a few seconds. "What's wrong?"

I shook my head. "Nothing. You look nice, that's all."

"No, I mean what's wrong with McKenzie?"

"Oh. I think she's hungry."

"Why didn't you feed her?" she asked.

"I was waiting for you to feed her."

"I don't have time to breastfeed her right now. I have to get to work."

"Oh. Okay. The baby formula is in the fridge, right?"

"I keep it on top of the fridge." She smiled at me, apologetically. "Sorry. I didn't know you were expecting me to feed her. Otherwise, I wouldn't have taken such a long shower."

"You can say that again," I muttered. Judges for the Husband of the Year award, please ignore that comment. I didn't mean it.

"Well, goodbye!" Brittany said. "Bye-bye, McKenzie! Be good for Daddy!"

"Bye, Mommy!" I said, waving McKenzie's arm at Brittany. I gave Brittany a kiss goodbye, and she left out the front door. A few seconds after that, McKenzie went back to screaming. "It's okay, you're going to have some formula." I carried her to the kitchen and put her down on the ground as I got the can of formula off of the fridge. She kicked her feet angrily. I couldn't blame her. If I was hungry, and somebody put me down instead of getting me food, I'd be angry, too. "Shhh...shhhh...It'll be ready soon."

The instructions said to mix two scoops of formula with four ounces of water, using the scoop in the formula can. Easy enough. I scooped the formula into the bottle, then I filled the bottle with the kitchen faucet. Instant formula!

Only it didn't work. I shook the bottle a bit, but all the formula powder stayed at the bottom. I checked the can of formula again, and this time, I noticed that you're supposed to put the water in *before* you put the formula.

"That's a stupid rule," I said.

McKenzie let out an angry cry. I'm guessing that means she agreed with me.

I put the bad bottle to the side for the moment, then filled a fresh bottle with four ounces of water. Luckily for me, they have the ounces marked on the side of baby bottles, because I have absolutely no idea how much water an ounce is. I filled the bottle with two scoops, accidentally spilling some of the powder on the counter. I put the lid on, shook the bottle firmly, and then picked up McKenzie and put the bottle in her mouth.

She opened her mouth eagerly and sucked on the bottle for a few seconds, before stopping and looking at me expectantly.

"Sorry, but that's the only kind of milk you're getting right now," I said.

She scrunched up her face, and I lightly pushed the bottle into her mouth before she started to scream again. This time, she decided that drinking from a bottle was okay, and she began sucking on it for real. I breathed a sigh of relief, then pulled out my phone.

McKenzie immediately stopped drinking from the bottle. She flapped her arms and started whimpering.

"What's wrong?" I asked.

She slapped my phone. I know it's an older model, but that's no reason to hit it!

I tried repositioning the phone out of McKenzie's reach, but she still grabbed for it. So then I tried repositioning her *and* the phone, but it didn't work. She refused to eat again until I put the phone away. I guess she wanted *all* of my attention.

I sat with her in my lap, until she was done eating. She started crying for another bottle, so I mixed more formula. After that one, she laid back on my lap and looked up at me, smiling. I noticed her mouth was covered with formula at this point, so I got a burp cloth and cleaned off her face.

Then I put the cloth on my shoulder and tried burping her. It didn't seem to work.

"Do you not have any burps?" I asked as I moved her to my other shoulder. Normally, she burped right away. Maybe I hadn't fed her correctly? Or she didn't have any gas in her—

McKenzie spit up on me, then she burped.

Ah. That was the reason for the holdup.

I took McKenzie with me to the bedroom and laid her on the bed to wait while I changed shirts. She put the burp cloth in her mouth. I figured that could be a choking hazard, so I took it out. McKenzie immediately started screaming.

"Ugh..." I groaned as I sat on my bed. I liked McKenzie, but this morning was turning out to be a disaster. How much longer until my wife came back?

I looked at the clock. It was only 8:15 AM.

I sighed. This was going to be a long day.

* * *

The good news is, infants are like bears. They don't do much besides eat and sleep (and poop). I played with her for ten minutes after her morning feeding, and then she went to sleep for fifteen minutes. After that, I changed her diaper, and she wanted me to carry her around the house for a while.

Luckily for me, Brittany came home early for lunch. That's the major benefit of having a job right in town: no hour-long bus commute into Portland. Looking back, that was the moment when my life changed forever.

"Did you have fun watching the baby?" Brittany asked.

I gave her a look that fully explained my thoughts on the situation.

"Oh. That's too bad. She seems like she's doing fine."

"She is, now that you're back home," I said. "I think she missed you."

"She'll have to get used to it."

"What's that supposed to mean?"

"Well...uh...I have some news! Big news," Brittany said. "My boss is planning to retire next month. And *her* boss quit when I was on maternity leave. So there are some vacancies at the top of the chain." Brittany waved her hand in a circle. "They want me to fill one of them."

"Fill—wait, you mean they—?"

"Yes! I got a promotion! Isn't that amazing?" Brittany seemed excited, and I couldn't blame her. She went in to quit, and they gave her a *promotion?* Some people have all the luck!

"That's great news!" I said. "Too bad you can't take it."

"It's not just a promotion. It's also a raise."

"Oh yeah? How much?"

She named a figure that was about thirty percent higher than I make.

"Are you *serious?* They must *really* want you to stick around!"

Brittany nodded. "I knew my boss liked me, but I didn't think she liked me *that* much! I told her I wanted to talk to you first before I accepted it."

"Gee, I dunno. This sounds like a great opportunity for you, but the timing is all wrong. Who would watch McKenzie while you're at work?"

"You would," Brittany said, pointedly. "I'll take the promotion, and you become the stay-at-home parent."

## Chapter 2

Losing my job was only *half* of my Weirdest Day Ever. There was still the whole "getting accused of murder" thing. Technically, that wouldn't happen until the next day, but I'm pretty sure "make yourself the prime suspect in a murder investigation" is not on anyone's to-do list.

It's strange. Normally, I would *love* the chance to be involved with a murder investigation. I mean, I've read all the *Harvey Brothers* mystery books! I've been with Fred and Jim Harvey as they solved every crime, even the really bad ones like *Mystery of the Mysterious Coin of Mystery*. (Seriously, who came up with that title? It's awful!)

But actually being accused of murder? Turns out it's not that much fun.

I'm getting ahead of myself, though.

"It's the only option that makes sense," Brittany said as she looked at me.

"Whoa, what?" I asked. "No way! I can't watch McKenzie full-time! I could barely handle watching her this morning!"

"Don't worry," Brittany said. "You'll get better at it with practice."

"I've had three months of practice being a dad already! I'm not as good with the baby as you are!"

"Look, we had it all figured out. I was going to be the stay-at-home parent, because I make less money. Now that *you're* the one making less money..." her voice drifted off.

She was right; I couldn't argue against that logic. That doesn't mean I didn't try. "Hold on a second. Maybe now you're making enough money to put us over the edge." I tried rebalancing our budget in my head. My monthly salary, plus her new monthly salary, minus the mortgage, minus the bills, minus food... "How much is daycare, again?"

"For newborns? Crazy expensive. We did the math already, remember? Paying for daycare would eat up most of your salary. It's not worth it to have one of us work full-time, for an extra hundred fifty a month. Besides, weren't you complaining about how awful your work is, yesterday?"

8

"Yeah, but just because I had a tough day at work doesn't mean I want to change careers!"

"Think of it this way," she said. "If you're at home every day, you'll have more free time to work on your Harvey Brothers videos!"

"You know those don't make a lot money."

"But at least you'd be making *some* money. It's better than nothing."

"Okay, okay, I'll think about it."

"What is there to think about?" She held McKenzie up to my face and talked in a baby voice. " 'I wanna stay with you all day, Daddy! Mommy is boring!' "

"Mommy is pushing it, after the worst morning ever," I warned, jokingly.

"What happened that was so bad?"

"She spit up on me!"

"She spits up on everyone. She's a baby."

"And it took forever to get the formula right! She screamed the whole time, too."

"Is that *all* that happened?" Brittany asked, with a skeptical look.

"It was way worse than it sounds," I said defensively.

Brittany put her hand on my shoulder. "Look, Ned. I get it. This is a lot to take in, all at once. But we have to do it. It's what's best for us and McKenzie."

"I know, it's just...a stay-at-home dad? Me? I'm not exactly the domestic type. I'm more of the awesome accountant type."

"You'll do fine. Trust me," Brittany said, as she kissed me. "I love you, Ned."

Now how could I say "no"' to that?

After lunch, I took the bus into work so I could tell my boss about my, uh...new full-time job. I spent most of the ride worrying that I couldn't

9

handle being a stay-at-home dad. I also looked up all of the daycares in town to see if it was at least *possible* to get McKenzie into one of them.

Bad news: All the daycares were booked solid for the year. The best I could do was sign up for a waiting list and hope to get lucky. I guess most people sign up for daycare *before* the baby is born, not three months after.

Worse news: Daycare easily cost more than I made. Clearly, I was in the wrong business! Daycare is where all the money's at.

So, Brittany was right. I would have to quit my job and she would be the one to keep working. It was the only plan that made financial sense. I just wish I had gotten some warning, before learning I had to spend the next five years at home.

Too bad none of our parents lived near us. I was sure Brittany's mom would volunteer to watch McKenzie for us on a full-time basis. I was fairly certain I could put up with seeing my mother-in-law every day, under those circumstances.

When I arrived at work, I went straight to the back of the building, where my boss' office was. My boss' name is Neil O'Neill. I know, stupid sounding name. Neil has a major chip on his shoulder because of it. The guy is unhappy in most circumstances, and I knew my bad news wasn't going to make him any happier.

I had just put my hand on the doorknob when someone grabbed me.

"Stop right there!"

It was Kelly Chang, Mr. O'Neill's secretary. She's—wait, you know what? Since we're talking about a murder mystery here, I'm going to do something I've always wanted to do: Suspect Dossiers! They have those in some of the *Harvey Brothers* books, and they're pretty awesome.

\* \* \*

*Suspect Dossier*

Name: Kelly Chang

Alias: The Punisher

Occupation: Officially, she's the office manager. Unofficially, she serves as my boss' angry bodyguard. It's her job to make sure no one hassles him.

Physical Description: Five feet four inches. Korean.

Marital Status: None of my business.

Hobbies: Scheduling, origami, sending nasty emails whenever someone takes the last cup of coffee without putting on a fresh pot.

Motive for Murder: Punishing someone for rule violations.

\* \* \*

"No one's allowed inside without—oh, hi, Ned," Kelly said. She put down the binder she was waving threateningly above her head. "Sorry. I didn't recognize you in street clothes. Are you sure you're allowed to wear those in here?"

"It doesn't really matter," I said.

Kelly narrowed her eyes. "Rules matter, Ned. I don't want to mark you up for a dress code violation."

I took a step backwards, without realizing it. Kelly had that effect on people. "I'm sorry. I just...I need to talk to Mr. O'Neill."

Kelly shook her head. "He told me not to let anyone disturb him today. Besides, you don't have an appointment."

"I know, but it's important."

She looked at me skeptically. "How important is it?"

"I'm quitting my job."

Kelly accidentally dropped her binder and quickly picked it up off the ground. "Seriously? This isn't a joke or anything, is it? Why are you quitting?"

"I'm...I'm going to be a stay-at-home dad."

"Seriously?" Kelly repeated. "*You?* You are going to be a stay-at-home-dad?" She was reacting like I said I was moving to Florida to become a full-time alligator wrestler.

11

"Yeah. Why? Do you think I can't handle it?"

"No, it's just that you...you're so..." Kelly stopped midsentence, then smiled at me. "This was your wife's idea, wasn't it?"

"Yes."

"She probably knows what she's doing."

I didn't like the sound of that. "What's that supposed to mean?"

"Nothing!" she said quickly. "You can go in and talk to him. Just try not to upset him, okay?"

I thanked Kelly and opened the door to Mr. O'Neill's office. He looked like he was playing on his phone, instead of working. When he saw me, he hastily put the phone away.

"Ned!" he barked. "Where were you this morning?"

"I took the morning off, Mr. O'Neill," I said.

"You didn't tell *me* about it!"

"I sent you an email about it last week."

"You should have *told* me about it, in person!" He grabbed his tie and clenched it. "We needed you here! Henderson sent in more spreadsheets today, and they're not going to summarize themselves!"

"Yes, sir. I mean, no sir. I mean..." I took a deep breath. "I'm here to turn in my two weeks' notice."

"WHAT?"

"I'm quitting my job. I know it's unexpected, but—"

"What possible reason could you have for quitting?!" he shouted. Pieces of spit flew out of his mouth as he did so. Gross.

"I need to take care of my daughter, so I'm becoming a stay-at-home dad."

"Your kid is ten years old. She can take care of herself! You can't fool me! You're leaving because you heard that rumor our business is going bankrupt. Well, stop your gossiping! *It's not true!*"

"Uh, no, my daughter is three months old," I said. "The company is having financial problems?"

"Not any more, it's not!" He grinned savagely, his teeth shining brighter than the light off his balding head. "But don't get any stupid ideas! Firing you is the easiest way for us to get more money in the budget, so stop joking around and *get back to work!*"

"I'm not joking! Today is my last day working for you!" I slammed my fist on the top of his desk, to emphasize how serious I was. I'll be honest, I've always wanted to slam my fist on the boss' desk and tell him I was quitting. I'm pretty sure *everyone* in our office has had that fantasy at one point or another.

"I thought you were turning in your two weeks' notice!" O'Neill said, triumphantly. "You're legally required to work for me for the next two weeks. And let me tell you, you're going to regret—"

"I'm going to use vacation time for that. I know I've got a lot of it built up."

"Your request for time off is *denied!* You didn't give me enough advance notice, and I don't do any favors for *quitters*. You're coming into office tomorrow, whether you like it or not!"

"You can't expect me to come into work with a three-month-old!"

"If you don't, you're fired!"

"But I just quit!"

"Then I'll hire you back, just to fire you!"

I rubbed my forehead. This was starting to sound like a dumb comedy routine. I decided to try a different tactic instead.

"Look, I'm sorry for all the problems that my resignation will cause," I said sympathetically. "It's not easy, having your entire life turned upside-down, trust me, *I know*, but I have to do this. My wife and I can't afford daycare for—"

"So the truth comes out! This is all just a trick to get a raise!" Strangely enough, he looked impressed with me. "While I appreciate your

13

underhanded business dealings, I would prefer that you use them on our *clients*, not me. Now get out of my office, or you're fired."

"You realize you've fired me three times in the past five minutes, right?" I asked. "Look, Mr. O'Neill, I'm not trying to cause problems for you. In fact, I'll probably need you to write a letter of recommendation for me after this is over. But due to circumstances beyond my control, I can no longer work at this company. I'm sorry this is so sudden."

"And I'm sorry I have such slow employees."

"Slow? Why are you calling me slow?"

"Not you, you idiot! I mean him!" He nodded to the person behind me. "What took you so long?"

"Sorry. I was on break," a deep voice said.

\* \* \*

*Suspect Dossier*

Name: Barry Wells

Alias: The scary-looking dude

Occupation: Security guard

Physical Description: Giant muscles, incredibly tall. Just based on looks alone, he almost *had* to become a security guard.

Biggest Secret: He has a baseball card collection of over 3,000 cards. After he told me that, he stopped seeming so scary.

Marital Status: Single, and he hates it.

Hobbies: Bowling, collecting baseball cards.

Motive for Murder: Someone looked at him funny.

\* \* \*

"Hi, Barry," I greeted him. "What brings you here?"

"You tell me," said Barry. "Someone in this office set off an alert for a hostile attacker."

I turned to Mr. O'Neill. He must have set off the alarm on his computer, while we were talking. "You called security on me? Really?"

"Barry, please escort this *ex-employee* out of the building," said O'Neill.

"You're fired?" asked Barry.

"I quit, actually," I said. "I'm going to be a stay-at-home dad."

"You? Really?"

"Yes. Is that so unbelievable?" I mean, I still didn't fully believe it myself, but it sounded worse when other people doubted it.

"It's just— you're a— no, man, it's cool," said Barry. "Let's go."

"Don't let the door hit you on the way out the building!" Mr. O'Neill snarled. He shot a triumphant grin at me as he locked the office door.

And that was the last time anyone saw Mr. O'Neill alive.

There was nothing else for me to do but leave the building. Considering how angry Mr. O'Neill was, I guess I was lucky I was able to leave without any injuries. Kelly apologized on the company's behalf and she promised to have all of my resignation paperwork taken care of by the end of the week.

I was feeling pretty crummy by the time I got home. That was the first time I had ever quit a job on purpose, and to make it worse, I was actually pretty good at the whole accounting thing! I mean, I wouldn't miss the hour-long commute into work every single day, but I would miss the feeling of being good at my job.

Not to say I'm bad at being a stay-at-home dad! I'm great at it! I think. Okay, so that morning had been borderline awful, but Brittany was right. I would get better at it with practice. And truth be told, I was looking forward to spending more time with McKenzie. So what if I messed up with making her baby formula? It was silly to think I'd be perfect at everything on the first try.

I tried looking up some stay-at-home dad tips on the trip home, when I noticed the acronym. Stay-At-Home Dad. SAHD. It sounded like "sad" for a reason. Why could SAHD not stand for something cooler, like "Someone's Awesome, High-income Dad"?

My sadness melted away when I entered the house and found that Brittany had bought me a cake. "It's to celebrate your new job," she said with a half-smile. I could tell she was feeling a little guilty about forcing me to quit without warning.

"Thanks," I said. "That's really nice of you."

"So, how did it go with Mr. O'Neill?"

"He fired me four times and called security to drag me out of the building. Other than that, I think he took it well."

Brittany's face fell. "I'm sorry."

"Don't be. I kind of expected it. Mr. O'Neill is a huge jerk. If I had to see him more than twice a month, I probably would have quit my job long ago."

"I really appreciate you doing this for me," Brittany said, as she kissed me. "It's nice to see how much you love me."

"I love you *and* McKenzie. And hey, we both knew going into this that marriage and having children would involve making sacrifices."

"True, but I still feel like I owe you big time for this," Brittany said. "I know if you asked *me* to quit my job unexpectedly, I'd be pretty angry with you."

"To be honest, I'm more worried than angry," I said. "What if I'm not a good stay-at-home dad? I mean, besides for McKenzie, my only experience with infants is reading *Harvey Brothers #127: The Kidnapped Baby-Sitters*."

Brittany looked confused. "What does that have to do with anything?"

"That's the book where the Harveys take care of an infant for two chapters. It's part of their trap, in order to catch the culprit."

"I highly doubt the Harvey Brothers are going to help you be a stay-at-home dad."

"Hey, you'd be surprised. Book three really helped me with my cooking!"

"It did not."

"Don't tell me you forgot! There was a full-page description of the most amazing meal; I knew I *had* to make it! The strips of freshly-cut meat, still moist with tenderness, layered below a thinly-sliced piece of cheddar which perfectly blended with a fragrant sauce of—"

"Ned, you made a ham sandwich."

"But it was an *awesome* ham sandwich," I clarified.

Brittany smiled at my silly joke. "Just promise me you'll take it easy with the experimental recipes. Now let's eat that cake!"

"Yum," I agreed.

# Chapter 3

I had a plan for my first official day as a stay-at-home dad. I was going to take McKenzie to the local baby playtime group. There, I would talk with all the other stay-at-home dads and ask them for advice. I had a few important questions that needed answering, like "what's the best way to change a baby without making a huge mess?", "how can you quickly figure out why the baby is crying?", and "is it possible to spend all day at home without going completely *insane*?"

Before I could do that, I needed to transport the baby from my house to the playgroup. That was when I met my new arch-nemesis. Something even worse than my crazy ex-girlfriend: the dreaded front pack.

If you've never heard of a front pack before, I envy you. It's a backpack-like device that's used for holding infants. It's sort of like carrying a baby in a kangaroo pouch, only the pouch is on your chest, and there is way too much Velcro involved. I took one look at it and knew putting it on would be impossible. There were two loops for each arm! Which one do you put your arm into?

I spent a few minutes struggling to figure it out myself before I got the manual. There were step-by-step instructions, showing all the ways to get a baby into a front pack. I couldn't help but notice that the model in the instructions used a baby doll, not a real baby. That did not exactly fill me with confidence.

*Step One: Hold your baby in front of you.* Simple enough.

*Step Two: Secure the belt around your waist.* I had no idea how I was supposed to do this while holding the baby.

*Step Three: Slip the right strap over your shoulder and tighten it.* Again, how was I to do this while holding a squirming infant? Unless I could levitate the baby with my mind, it wasn't going to work.

*Step Four* had me tighten the straps on the straps, because of *course* there were straps on straps. I imagined next that there would be more straps upon straps.

By *Step Five*, I noticed the baby was suddenly facing the opposite direction. Or maybe I had it backwards? No, the baby had definitely switched directions. Clearly, I was supposed to use telekinesis to rotate my child. I suppose lowering them from the sky with a floating elevator was also an option.

*Step Six* required me to put two straps together in the middle of my back. I have a hard enough time reaching that part of my back normally. Trying to reach it with a child on my chest would be impossible. To make matters worse, the straps only connected if I put three hooks together in a specific order. Because why *not* use the complicated lock for the strap that you're physically incapable of seeing?

By the time I reached *Step Seven*, I had given up. Good thing I had tried doing it by myself, first. If I had tried doing it with McKenzie, she probably would have gotten hurt.

"Daddy has no idea what he's doing," I told her.

She smiled at me.

I tried undoing all the straps, pulling them out to the maximum length. Then I put the various clips together before putting the front pack on my body. Believe it or not, that seemed to work. I slipped McKenzie in through the top, then tightened the straps.

"I did it," I said proudly.

The baby slipped down three inches and started crying.

"Oh no! No, no, no! Here—try to—grrrr..." I grunted, as I tried to get her into the ideal location. Apparently, I had to set the front pack about four inches above my waist, to get it to work properly. The chest area was still somewhat loose, no matter what I tried. Either these things were designed for female bodies, or my wife had gotten a larger size because she's taller than me.

"Next time, we're using the stroller," I decided.

McKenzie rested with her head against my chest. Because I couldn't see her face, I started to worry that I would accidentally suffocate her. I tried holding a finger up to her nose, to feel her exhaling. She opened her mouth and tried to suck on my finger.

"Yeah, you're fine," I said.

I should probably note that I had never been to baby playtime before. My wife was the one who went regularly. She said the other people in the group were really nice, the babies had a great time, and besides, it was free. Those were all very good reasons. Also, it was the perfect excuse for getting out of the house. Staying inside all day would have driven me crazy.

The baby playtime group was at the local community center by the mall, if you can call five stores "a mall." Lincoln Lake isn't exactly the largest town in the Portland Metro Area. Brittany and I live here because it's where we both grew up, but most people live here because it's an hour bus ride away from Portland.

The flyer by the front desk said baby playtime was in room 2A. After a little searching, I found a door labelled "2A" and stepped inside. Immediately, five women turned to eye me suspiciously, like I wasn't supposed to be there. Was I in the right room?

"Hello?" a woman asked. "Are you lost?"

I looked around. The walls had colorful pictures of flowers and animals, definitely designed for younger children. The women were sitting in a large circle, around a carpet. Six babies were lying on the carpet. I decided this *had* to be the right place.

"Hi," I said. "I'm here for baby playtime?"

The women looked at each other, unsure of what to do.

The one woman I guessed was in charge said, "I'm sorry, but we've been doing this for several months now. I believe we have a new session opening up in the spring, if you're interested."

"No, we're not new. I mean, *I'm* new, but the baby isn't. Well, technically, all babies are *new*, but..." I stopped and mentally scolded myself for babbling like an idiot. Why was I feeling so nervous? And why weren't there any other dads here?

"I'm McKenzie's father. My wife Brittany told me to come here."

"*Oh!* We know McKenzie!" the leader woman said. "We *love* McKenzie! It's so nice of you to help drop her off, isn't it, ladies?"

The other women nodded and gave general murmurs of assent.

"I wish *my* husband would help do the baby chores," one said.

"But where's Brittany?" the leader asked. "This isn't a dump and run group. One parent must be with the child at all times. Is Brittany still in the car?"

"No, she's not here today. It's just me."

"What happened to her?" one woman asked, with an unnecessary amount of viciousness.

"She's finished with maternity leave. I'm the stay-at-home parent now."

"That's, um...different," the leader woman said. "Well, have a seat, and we'll get started in a few minutes. We can go around the room and introduce ourselves for any, uh, newcomers."

Everyone stared at me, and I started to feel like I was part of a police lineup. Why didn't Brittany tell me that baby playtime was a women-only thing? This was awkward. Like, junior high gym class awkward.

I sat down and started to undo the front pack. Naturally, it refused to cooperate. I couldn't reach the strap in the back, and when I pulled the one on the side, McKenzie screamed suddenly. I think it was pinching her arm.

"Do you need some help?" the woman next to me asked.

"No, I've got it," I said. No way was I going to admit I didn't know how to work the front pack, in front of a group of strangers. That would be almost as embarrassing as asking one of the other moms to unzip me. I played with the side strap for about five seconds, before realizing it was pointless.

I stood up again to give myself more space, then I undid the strap on the far side, which had somehow gotten stuck under the belt part. I did my best to pretend that everything was totally normal, like I stood up to grab at my own butt all the time. Luckily, the front pack cooperated this time, and I was able to pull McKenzie out.

I put her on the floor in front of me, then looked around the room. There were six moms there. The leader was wearing yoga pants and a purple headband that matched her workout top. I was mildly impressed. My workout clothes are a ratty old t-shirt and basketball shorts that I've had for ten years. No way could I wear them in public without looking ridiculous.

Next to her were two moms with matching striped sweaters and jeans. They even had similar hairstyles. Gee, if there was another dad in the group, maybe he and I could coordinate our outfits, too. That'd be cute.

There was a large woman with messy hair and a t-shirt with birds all over it. She was the only one there who didn't make me feel nervous, mostly because she was asleep. Her back rested against a pillar, and she was snoring softly.

On my left was a woman with the most ridiculous hair I've ever seen. The right half was draped forward over her head, like she was trying to cover up her eye. The left half was pulled backwards. I suppose it was an interesting look, but I got the impression that one side of her head was trying to escape from the other side.

Next to her was a—Brittany, please don't read this part—a hot babe in a skinny top and skinny jeans, and wow, she was way too skinny to have given birth recently. Or ever, really. Her thick red hair fell across her shoulders in silky waves, sort of like the mermaid picture that we have in McKenzie's room.

The good-looking woman brought a hand to her large chest and ran her fingers along her soft skin. My eyes almost popped out of my head, as she grabbed the top of her outfit and gently tugged down. *What is she doing? That's not—Oh no! She's going to breastfeed. OH NO! Look away, Ned! LOOK AWAY!*

Just in time, I looked away from Movie Star Mom and started staring at Sleeping Woman's shoe. That shoe had suddenly become the most fascinating thing in the world to me. I watched her baby crawl around near her feet, and I realized McKenzie was the only baby in the group that couldn't crawl yet. I hoped that wouldn't be a problem.

No one else showed up in the next few minutes, and when it was eleven o'clock, Workout Mom sat up straight.

"Okay, it's *time* to *start! Hello*, everyone! I'm *Sara* Benson, and it's *nice* to *see you* today!" she squealed loudly. "So, let's *go around the room* and say *who we are!*"

Uh oh. She was one of those people who talk strangely around babies. I mean, I'm normally fine with baby talk, but Workout Mom sounded like she was trying to sing every other word.

The first to speak was one of the women in matching sweaters. "I'm Jennifer, and this is Claudia. She's six months." She gestured to her twin. "This is my friend, Jennifer. Her baby is also named Claudia."

"It's such a cool name," the other Jennifer replied. "When I heard you'd picked it, I knew I had to pick it, too."

Suddenly, I remembered these two women. Back when I was in school, there was a class three years ahead of me, which had five Jennifers in it. Everyone called them "The Jennifers", because they were together all the time. Apparently, that hadn't changed, now they were adults.

Sleeping Woman didn't say anything, so I figured it was my turn. "I'm Ned, and this is McKenzie. She's three months old. I, uh...huh. I used to be an accountant, but now I'm the stay-at-home dad." I paused, but no one said anything. The silence stretched on for several uncomfortable seconds, until I turned to Crazy Hair and said, "You're next, Cra—Cruh—you're next."

She gave me a weird look, before introducing herself and her eight-month old son. A son? I guess that means I wasn't the only male in the room after all. Then Movie Star Mom had a long, foreign name that I had never heard of before. I'm kind of awful at names, in case you couldn't tell, so I decided to keep thinking of her as Movie Star Mom.

"Okay!" said Workout Mom. "Then, *let's get started!* First is the *Hello Babies* song!"

Things went pretty smoothly once class started, mostly because I didn't have to talk to anyone. All I had to do was sing to the babies and make hand gestures. I didn't know half of the hand gestures, but that's okay. I'm pretty sure the babies didn't know them, either.

The playtime was made up of six songs. Workout Mom criticized me for not singing loud enough, saying I "wasn't a team player." When I took a solo on the next song, she told me to go back to singing quietly.

I guess the babies liked it enough. After that, Workout Mom pulled out a multi-colored parachute. We fluttered it up and down, while singing a song about parachutes and wind. Then, we laid the babies down on top of the parachute.

"Everyone *grab a side* and walk in *a big circle!*" Workout Mom said.

It was actually pretty cool. We spun the parachute in a big circle, dragging the babies along. McKenzie was too young to notice anything out of the ordinary, but some of the older babies loved it. I was starting to think things were going great, when I tripped on Sleeping Woman's foot.

Yes, she was still sleeping, even though she had spent the last twenty-plus minutes in a room with singing parents. I wish *I* could sleep that soundly, but sadly, I live with an infant who likes to kick me in her sleep, to make sure I'm still there.

I tripped over Sleeping Woman's feet, accidentally jerking the parachute. All the babies were jostled and started screaming. As I fell over, I pushed Crazy Hair out of the way and smashed into Movie Star Mom's legs. Both women stumbled backwards, but unlike me, they weren't klutzy enough to fall down.

"Oh no! Are you okay?" Jennifer #1 asked.

I rubbed my arm. "Yeah, I think I— "

"Not *you*! I meant *Claudia!*" Jennifer #1 picked up her baby and started rocking her. The other moms collected their children and soothed them. Movie Star Mom gave me a nasty look, like I purposely knocked her over for fun. I sighed and picked up McKenzie, who was crying like the others. She soothed herself by sucking on one of my fingers.

Workout Mom put away the parachute. "I think we should sing the *goodbye* song," she said, with a glance at me. I got the hint.

The goodbye song wasn't going to win a Grammy anytime soon. Here are the lyrics:

*Goodbye babies*
*Goodbye babies*
*Goodbye babies*
*Goodbye babies*

After that, we sang the mommy version of the song, which is the same thing, only it's "Goodbye mommies." Workout Mom started to say something else, but then she stopped and forced us to sing the daddy version of the song. I appreciated the effort to include me, but it actually made me feel embarrassed. There weren't any other dads there. Just me. I didn't need a whole song all for myself.

Workout Mom brought out toys for the babies to play around with. She explained to everyone—which meant she explained to *me*, because everyone else already knew what they were doing—that playtime officially ran from 11:00 to 11:30, but they normally kept the room open until 12. That way, the babies could play by themselves for a while, and the parents would have an opportunity to talk to each other.

I didn't know how long McKenzie wanted to play, but I knew that I wanted to get out as soon as possible before I embarrassed myself again. I checked McKenzie's diaper—stinky—and I used it as an excuse to leave right away.

I made it as far as the bathroom door, before I realized that I had left McKenzie's diaper bag in the playroom. I went back to get it, only to find the moms having a conversation about how they first learned they were pregnant.

"Sam and I were trying for *months* to get pregnant," Jennifer #1 said. "I was checking practically every week."

The other Jennifer said, "And once *Jennifer* told me that she was pregnant, I *knew* I had to get pregnant, too."

25

"I'm so glad we were pregnant at the same time," Jennifer said. "There's no way I could have done it alone."

"Oh, I know! Being pregnant at the same time as your best friend is *such* a help. It's brought us closer as friends."

So the Jennifers both got pregnant in tandem. Is this normal human behavior? I wonder if the other three Jennifers were in on the pregnancy plan.

"Well, we weren't trying to get pregnant," Movie Star Mom said. "So we didn't realize it, until later into the pregnancy. I didn't have morning sickness; I was sick all day. It took me three weeks of being sick before I went to the doctor, and she told me I was pregnant."

Crazy Hair turned and looked at me. "How did you find out?"

I was a little startled to be included in the conversation. "What?"

"How did you find out your wife was pregnant?" she repeated slowly.

"I found out when my wife marched out of the bathroom and threw a pregnancy test at my head," I said. "She said that I...uh...never mind."

The moms looked at me like I was crazy. Yep. It was *definitely* time to leave. I put McKenzie in the front pack, made a big show of having her wave goodbye to her friends, then I ran out the door.

I immediately had to readjust the front pack because the stupid thing wasn't on correctly. I shook my head, mad at my mistakes with the front pack and the baby playtime group. This stay-at-home dad thing wasn't working out as well as I'd hoped.

We went back home where I fed McKenzie, and she went straight to sleep. I read for a little bit, when I was interrupted by my phone ringing. I didn't recognize the number, but it had a Portland area code, so I knew it was from somewhere nearby.

"Hello?" I answered.

"Hello, this is Detective Dodd of the Portland Police," said a voice with the slightest hint of a French accent, on the other end of the line. "Is this Ned Gray?"

"Uh...yes, that's me. Is something wrong?"

"You could say that," Dodd said wryly. "Your boss was murdered last night. I'd like you to come in for questioning."

# Chapter 4

It's amazing how much faster it is to get to work when it's the middle of the day, compared to taking the bus during rush hour. I'd probably do it every day if parking downtown didn't cost stupid amounts of money. I'm talking "infant daycare" levels of money.

The first area inside of the building where I work—where I *used* to work, I mean—is a big waiting room. In order to reach the area where the workers are, you have to go through the doors by the security desk, where Barry was seated when I came in.

"Hey," he said. He looked at McKenzie. "Is that the baby?"

"Yes."

Barry let out a low whistle. "Dang, that kid looks just like you. You sure it's not a boy?"

"Oh, I'm sure." I had changed too many diapers to have any doubts about her gender. Seven diapers in the last day in a half. Or was it eight?

"The police officer's waiting for you in the Burnside Conference Room. I'll escort you there."

"That's not necessary. I know where it is."

"Yeah, but all non-employees need a security escort. Those are the rules." Barry shrugged. "Kelly won't let me break them, even for you."

I pretended he was talking about escorting McKenzie, not me, although I probably should have taken it as a compliment that he thought I was a legitimate security risk.

Barry swiped his keycard and opened the doors for us. I carried McKenzie in my arms as I followed him to the Burnside Conference Room. For a conference room, it's pretty small. At most, three chairs and a desk can fit inside. It mostly gets used for annual performance reviews. And now, murder interrogations.

Detective Dodd was already inside, waiting for me. He was tall with a large forehead, made all the larger by the fact that he was balding. His nose looked like it had once been broken. "So you're Ned Gray."

I nodded. "And this is McKenzie." I held her up.

"Why'd you bring a baby with you?"

"It's *my* baby," I said, a tad defensively.

"No need to get upset. I wasn't accusing you of stealing her, if that's what you were thinking," Dodd said. Grimly, I wondered if he normally accused people of crimes they didn't commit. "You're watching her today, I take it."

"Uh...today and *every* day," I said. "I'm a stay-at-home dad now."

"You quit your high-paying job in order to be a baby-sitter?"

I decided to lighten the mood with a joke. "Trust me, it was *not* high-paying, and it's not baby-sitting if it's your own kid."

"Is that right?"

"Yeah. You know the difference between parents and baby-sitters?"

"What?"

"Baby-sitters get paid," I smiled.

Instead of laughing at my joke, Dodd scowled. Clearly, he was the angry, no-nonsense type of policeman. The Harvey Brothers ran into those a lot. Luckily, they always tend to have friendly assistants who have no problem giving the Harveys top secret information on the case.

"Do you have an assistant or someone else I could work with, perhaps?" I asked hopefully. Maybe someone more cheerful?

"No, I do not! Now *sit down!*"

I immediately sat down and shut up. Detective Dodd nodded his approval and tapped for a bit on a laptop that was on the desk. "Now tell me about your movements yesterday."

I resisted the urge to make a dumb joke about dance moves. "I watched the baby all morning while my wife went in to work. Her maternity leave ended this week. The plan was that she would quit her job and continue being a stay-at-home mom, but when she came home from lunch, she told me that she had gotten a promotion. So *I* ended up being the one who had to quit their job to watch the baby full-time."

"Interesting," Dodd said. He typed up some notes. "So your wife got an unexpected promotion?"

"Very unexpected. She just got back from maternity leave. You don't really expect to get a promotion first thing after you've been gone for months."

"And did she show you any proof of this promotion?"

"Proof? What, like a letter from human resources?" I shook my head. "No, she didn't get anything like that."

"So, you don't know for sure she actually got the promotion?"

"I trust my wife, Detective Dodd," I said seriously. "If she says she got a promotion, she got a promotion. She wouldn't lie about something like that, just to get out of being the stay-at-home parent."

Dodd grunted noncommittally and typed furiously for a few seconds. I hope he wasn't writing "Ned is a gullible idiot" in his case notes.

McKenzie grabbed at my shirt and cooed softly. I adjusted her in my arms and put my pinky finger in her mouth, to keep her occupied. She sucked on it gently.

"What happened next?" Dodd asked.

"My wife watched the baby, while I came here."

"When was this?"

"I don't know. Sometime after one o'clock? I didn't check how quickly the bus was going. I was a little preoccupied with the whole 'I'm going to quit my job' thing."

"I can check the bus records. What happened after the bus arrived?"

"I entered the building like normal and went straight to Mr. O'Neill's office." I paused. "No, wait. I talked with Kelly first. She told me I couldn't go in to see the boss without a good reason, so I told her I was quitting. She let me in after that. Neil was, uh...playing on his phone instead of working. Not to speak ill of the dead of course."

"How did the victim react when you told him you were quitting?" Dodd asked.

I didn't like the sound of the word "victim". It made Mr. O'Neill's death seem...I dunno, more *real* somehow.

"He was beyond furious," I said. "He yelled at me for several minutes, and he also threatened to fire me multiple times. Like, the only time he *didn't* yell was when he thought I was angling to get a raise. That was kind of weird."

"So, you and the victim had an altercation, shortly before his death. Did it turn violent?"

I didn't like the sound of that, either. "Whoa, whoa. When you put it *that* way, I sound like a murder suspect."

"You're a person of interest in this case," Dodd said simply.

"That's what the ladies tell me."

"Answer the question!" he snapped, scowling again. I guess he didn't like my dad jokes.

"No, it didn't turn violent. I left the room peacefully. You said he died shortly afterwards? When did he die?"

"I'm still waiting on the autopsy results. His body was discovered at 5:30 p.m.. Nobody has admitted to entering Mr. O'Neill's office after you left."

"Five thirty," I repeated. That was good news for me. "That's a four-hour window. Plenty of time for another person to come in and commit the crime."

"I can do the math on my own, thanks."

"Just trying to help. I've always wanted to solve a mystery in real life."

"Watching crime dramas on TV does *not* make someone qualified to solve mysteries," Dodd sighed. "This is a little more complicated than 'The Case of the Missing Diaper'."

Wow. Sarcasm, much? "Sorry, I just...never mind. But for the record, I'd like to state that I'm innocent. I didn't kill my boss."

"Can you prove that?" Detective Dodd asked.

"I...yes! I have an alibi—Barry! He escorted me out of the building after I talked with Mr. O'Neill. Ask him! He'll tell you that O'Neill was still alive when we left the office!"

"I already talked with him about that, actually. His story matches up with yours."

"See? I'm innocent!"

"Not necessarily. You could have snuck back into the office later and killed him. As you said, there was a four-hour window."

"That's impossible. You can't enter the building without going past Barry's security station. He would have seen me, if I re-entered."

"Normally, that's true, but Barry tells me that he took a fifteen minute break yesterday afternoon. You could have circumvented security by entering the building when he was gone."

Well, *that* was inconvenient timing. Also, it wasn't reassuring to know that our building's security doesn't work whenever the guard goes on break. But I wasn't about to take the blame for Mr. O'Neill's death, just because my co-worker went on break.

"Come on, how am I supposed to know ahead of time when Barry takes his breaks? Fifteen minutes in a four-hour gap is...um...I can't do that math in my head, but it's less than ten percent. The odds of me guessing it correctly are pretty low."

"True, but you're familiar with Mr. Wells. Who's to say you don't know his normal schedule?" The look on Detective Dodd's face clearly indicated he thought my innocence was as likely as snow in July.

"You could ask him yourself." I was pretty sure he'd back me up. Or at least, the autopsy results would. Like I said, the odds of anything happening in that particular fifteen-minute gap were pretty slim.

"That I will," Dodd said. "You know your co-workers better than I do, Mr. Gray. Who do *you* think is the culprit?"

"Uh..." I tried to think of who had a good motive for killing Mr. O'Neill, but I came up blank. "I don't know anyone who's particularly close to him. In fact, I mostly avoided him. He wasn't the nicest boss ever...but he mentioned the company's been having financial problems lately. Could his death have something to do with that?"

"You think he was killed by an angry client? Possible, I suppose, but I suspect this one is an inside job. No outsider would know how to get past security."

"Then I'd have to guess Kelly. I don't want to accuse her, but she's the one who had the most day-to-day contact with Mr. O'Neill. Plus, her desk is right outside his office. If anyone had a good chance of getting into his office unseen, it was her."

"She *also* claims to have taken a long, unscheduled break yesterday afternoon," Dodd said, thoughtfully. I couldn't believe it. Was this just bad timing, or did *everyone* in the office go on break whenever they felt like it? I wish they would have told *me* about this unofficial company policy. It would have made my job less stressful, that's for sure.

"One final question," Dodd said. "What happened to the paperwork for your dismissal?"

"The paperwork for my dismissal?" I repeated. "Kelly said she would send it to me, but I never got it. I guess she was distracted by the murder and everything. Why do you ask?"

"It went missing," Dodd said simply.

"Missing? How can it go missing, if I never got it?"

"*You* never got it. O'Neill did. The computer says the last thing printed in his office was a copy of your dismissal papers. But when we searched the room, we didn't find them anywhere."

That didn't sound good. Either it was an honest mistake, or the culprit took the papers with them in order to frame me.

"Uh...maybe Mr. O'Neill left his office at one point?" I guessed.

"The door was locked from the inside when the body was discovered, and Barry confirmed that the victim locked the door after the two of you left the room."

"Yeah, I remember that, but you can't honestly believe the door to Mr. O'Neill's office was locked for four hours straight. Locked room murder mysteries don't happen in real life. The culprit must have come in, killed Mr. O'Neill, then locked the room after they exited, that's all."

"That's my working theory. But I'm still interested in those missing papers. As far as I'm concerned, you're the only person here who would have a reason to take them."

"I didn't do it, Detective Dodd. I have a baby to worry about." I gestured to McKenzie, who yawned at me. "I don't have the time or the energy to plot complicated murders."

"If you say so. That's all of the questions I have for now, but I'll almost certainly have more questions for you once the results come in from the lab. How long can you stay?"

I didn't have to be home until my wife got off of work, so I suppose I could have stayed for a few hours, but I wanted to be out of there as soon as possible, before I got arrested on false charges.

"McKenzie? You want to stay here for the rest of the day?" I turned her around so she was standing upright, facing Detective Dodd. As I did so, I secretly pinched her backside. She screamed loudly. A mean trick, I know, but it was better than staying here and getting badgered by a grumpy policeman. "Sounds like a 'no.' I'd better get back home. It was, uh, interesting meeting you, Detective Dodd."

Dodd grunted in response.

I got up and left the room as quickly as I could. In retrospect, that probably wasn't the greatest idea. I should have stayed and asked for more details about the crime, like what the murder weapon was. I mean, Dodd probably wouldn't have told me anything, but it couldn't have hurt to ask.

Barry was waiting for me outside the door. "All done?"

"Gosh, I hope so," I said. "That officer thinks *I* did it just because I'm last person to see O'Neill alive. Is there some sort of record of who goes in and out of his office?"

"The boss didn't keep a visitor's log. Wouldn't be helpful, if he did. No one's gonna come in, kill a man, then sign his visitor's log." He had a point there.

"I guess, but what about—hey. This isn't the way to the exit. This is the way to—"

"Kelly's desk," Barry said. "She wanted to talk to you before you left the building. Said it was important."

Well, that didn't sound good. Today was just not my day.

Barry led me straight to Kelly's workspace. As I told Detective McGrumpyPants, her desk is right outside Mr. O'Neill's office. I could see police crime scene tape, stretched across the office door. If I hadn't been preoccupied with the fact that I was a murder suspect, I probably would have thought it was cool to see police tape in real life.

"Ned. You're late," Kelly snapped. "You were supposed to be here five minutes ago. I've got a client call scheduled for now."

"Sorry?" I said, the word coming out as a question. What else was I supposed to say? I had no idea she wanted to see me, and besides, I was kind of busy being interrogated by a police detective.

"Good to see you're not in handcuffs yet. Now about—is that the *baby?* Oh my gosh, she's just the cutest! Let me hold her! Let me hold her!"

"Uh, sure," I said, handing McKenzie over to Kelly. "Her name is McKenzie."

"Who's a good girl? Who's a good girl?" Kelly cooed. "You are! Peekaboo! Ha ha ha! Peekaboo!" McKenzie smiled and made noises at her. Believe it or not, this was normal behavior for some people. When they see a baby for the first time, they treat it like some kind of dog.

I glanced at Barry, and he rolled his eyes.

Kelly's playtime came to an abrupt end when the phone rang.

"Crap, that's the client," she said. She gave the baby back to me and pointed to an empty cardboard box on the floor. "Clean out your cubicle, okay? We'll talk later."

"But I wanted to know—" I began to say, but it was too late. Kelly was already on the phone, talking in a high-pitched, friendly voice. I was impressed by her ability to change personality traits on a dime. She looked at me and made a dismissive gesture, so I left for my cubicle.

The co-worker in the next cube over leaned backwards to see me. "Ned! Is it true you're getting arrested?"

* * *

*Suspect Dossier*

Name: Alan Stacker

Alias: Nerd City

Occupation: Accountant

Physical Description: Heavyset, with a nose that looks permanently smashed, because of the large glasses he always wears.

Marital Status: Married with two kids.

Annoyance Factor: 10 out of 10. He never knows when to shut up.

Hobbies: Interfering in other people's business, interrupting my lunches, and making jokes about the day of the week.

Motive for Murder: He's easily frightened, and Mr. O'Neill was pretty intimidating. If Alan thought he was in danger from Mr. O'Neill, who knew how far he'd go to protect himself?

* * *

"No, I'm not being arrested," I said.

"But you *are* fired, right? That's good. I mean, not good that you're being fired, obviously—although they'll probably let me move into your cube now, so that's a bonus—but good that you're not in jail for killing Neil, and hey, is that your baby or your clone? Ha! She should come over and play with *my* toddler for a while! If you're not in jail anymore."

Believe it or not, Alan talked like that normally. I was used to it at this point. The trick is to focus one of his statements and ignore all the others.

"Yes, I'm not working here anymore," I said. "I'm going to be a stay-at-home dad from now on."

"Better you than me. I'd *hate* having to watch my kids all the time. Talk about a Terrible Day Tuesday! Ha!"

"If you say so."

"I can't believe Neil is dead! I came into work this morning, and I was all, 'What? What do you mean the boss is dead?' Too bad it didn't happen on a Favorite Day Friday, huh? Then we'd get a three-day weekend, ha! Although I guess it's already like a weekend because nobody's getting any work done. Who can concentrate, knowing we have a murderer in our office? I bet it's the same person who steals lunches from the fridge."

"Do you know *how* he was killed?" I asked.

"I heard he was bludgeoned with one of those three-hole punch machines." Alan shuddered, causing his half-done tie to flop against his chest. "Killed with office supplies. Horrible way to go."

I thought for a second. I was fairly certain I saw one of those machines on O'Neill's desk yesterday. "Was it *his* three-hole punch?"

"Duh! What, you think the culprit brought their own three-hole punch with them? Talk about a *dead giveaway!* But seriously, I wish they would let me keep a three-hole punch at my desk. I'm tired of going to the supply room just to get things to fit in my binders."

Hm. If Mr. O'Neill was killed with his own three-hole punch, that definitely made it seem like it wasn't premeditated. That probably let me off the hook! I mean, Dodd was accusing me of sneaking back into the

37

building. That's premeditation, right there. Unless the murder was like *Harvey Brothers #415: The Tax Fraud Scandal* when the culprit purposely fixed the scene to make it look like a crime of passion.

"I'd like to take a look at the supply room, if you don't mind," I said.

"Nope," said Barry, "no playing detective. Once you're done, you're outta here. Otherwise, Kelly will chew my head off. Besides, the police already checked there. No one's been inside, as far as we can tell."

"Ooo, you think you can solve the mystery?" Alan asked. "It's just like those Harvey Brothers books you always read! Except this one is an actual murder, instead of stupid mysteries like missing pets and stuff."

"They are *not* stupid books!" I exclaimed. "And besides, the Harveys solve murder mysteries all the time in the 1980's Super Harvey Brothers series."

"Is that the one where they meet hot babes all the time?" Alan asked.

"...You're gonna have to be more specific," I said. The Harveys met attractive women in pretty much *every* book series.

"Wish I could meet a hot babe," Barry said. "This stupid job cuts into all my time. They *really* need to hire another guard."

"Oh, I know!" Alan said. "My wife is always complaining about how I work too late. I tried asking O'Neill if I could change my hours, but all he said was if I didn't finish all my work during the week, I should come in on weekends. As if! Talk about Suffering Saturday!"

Alan and Barry both had problems with O'Neill forcing them to work too much? Interesting. That sounded like a motive!

"And where were you, yesterday afternoon?" I asked casually.

"I was busy at my desk all day," Alan said.

"Busy doing what?"

"Not committing murder," Barry said.

"Oh, me too!" Alan said. "Not committing violent felonies is the greatest. I do it all the time."

"I know you like those mystery books," Barry said, "but this ain't the time to play detective. I already had *one* interrogation today. I'm not gonna put up with another. Now finish packing your stuff and leave, or I'll do it for you."

I groaned. Yeah, it made sense that they wouldn't let the prime murder suspect be the lead investigator on the case, but this was totally unfair. A chance to solve a real-life mystery, and wasn't allowed to take it? How was I ever going to prove my innocence?

I didn't get a chance to ask any more questions, as Barry took me directly to the exit once my cardboard box was full with my belongings. Have you ever tried carrying a baby, a diaper bag, and a box full of work supplies, all at the same time? It's almost impossible.

My sleuthing skills weren't defeated *that* easily, though. When no one was looking, I "accidentally" dropped my credit card in my cube. That way, I'd have a good excuse to come back and snoop around some more.

...Either that, or someone would steal my card and buy a bunch of stuff with it. I hoped that wouldn't happen.

# Chapter 5

I took McKenzie home, and we played with blocks until she fell asleep. I was tempted to fall asleep, too. It had been a stressful day.

Brittany came home a few hours later. The first thing she did was sit on the couch and take her hair out of her ponytail. I personally think she looks better with her hair down, but she disagrees with me. I'm sure we'll have lots of fun revisiting the conversation about hairstyles when McKenzie's hair grows out, because Brittany once said McKenzie would look great with a pumpkin top. I think the only thing sillier than a pumpkin top is wearing an actual pumpkin on your head.

Brittany said she was full, and she had to feed McKenzie right away. I handed over the baby to her, and I sat down next to her. People say it's hard to talk to your spouse when you've got a baby, but I've found the exact opposite to be true. It's super easy to have a conversation with your wife when she's sitting down and can't get up for twenty minutes.

"How was going back to work?" I asked. "Do you remember everything? Is it just like riding a bicycle?"

"Not really," Brittany said. "I have to learn all this new managerial stuff, but it's not too tough yet because the official training sessions begin next week. I'm mostly just coasting for now. How was *your* day?"

"It was basically the worst day ever."

"You said that yesterday."

"Yeah, but I mean it this time," I said. "Baby playtime was a disaster, I can't figure out how to use the front pack, and I'm now the prime suspect in a murder investigation."

"You killed the front pack? Cute."

"No, I'm serious. Mr. O'Neill was killed after I quit yesterday."

"WHAT?" Brittany shouted. McKenzie started screaming, upset.

"Sorry! Didn't mean to disturb you! But yes, I got a call from the police today. They asked me to come into work, so I could answer some questions."

"Wow, that's crazy. You *have* to tell me more," Brittany said.

"I told you that Mr. O'Neill yelled at me, and he had the security guard eject me from the building, right?" I asked.

"Yeah."

"Well, he didn't come out of his office after that. He stayed inside until his dead body was found, four hours later."

"Who found the body?" Brittany asked.

"Gosh, I don't know. The detective didn't share all the details with me. But he *did* say that Kelly the office manager took a long break at some point that afternoon."

"You think she did it?"

"Maybe. I was trying to say that she was gone long enough for someone to enter the office, kill O'Neill, then leave without being seen. Actually, Barry the security guard also took a fifteen-minute break that afternoon, so I guess there were *two* opportunities for someone to sneak in and kill Mr. O'Neill."

Brittany shook her head. "Wow, your office security is awful. But why do they think *you* did it?"

"I think it's because I was the last person to see Mr. O'Neill alive. Plus, we just had a huge fight where he yelled at me a lot. That looks suspicious, you know?"

"Yeah, but you have an alibi. Me! I was here when you got home yesterday."

"That's right, I should have remembered that! I'll tell the detective if he asks me again."

"Hm..." Brittany said, thinking.

"What is it?"

41

"If I could play devil's advocate here, your alibi isn't perfect." She smiled, then pretended to look suspiciously at me. "You got home a half-hour late, remember? Who's to say you didn't use that half-hour to kill someone?"

"Shoot," I said. She was right. I had forgotten that I got home late that day. "I swear, if I get arrested because of bad traffic, I am never using the bus system again."

Brittany laughed. "I'm sure it won't be an issue. When did he die?"

"I have no idea. Like I said, the detective didn't give me all the details of the case."

"That's a bummer. Do you know how he died?"

"The murder weapon was a three-hole punch machine, taken from the victim's desk," I said. "Almost anyone could have used it."

"He was killed with a three-hole punch?" Brittany winced. "Ouch. That sounds really painful. Remind me not to have one of those in my office."

"I don't want to think about it. The entire thing makes me queasy. I haven't had dinner yet, you know."

"Yeah, I was going to ask about that. Where's dinner?"

That question confused me, since Brittany had made dinner every night for the past two months. "I don't know. Why are you asking me? I thought *you* were going to make it."

Brittany gave me an annoyed look. "We went over this last night. You're the stay-at-home parent, so *you* have to make the meals."

"Oh, is *that* what you meant? Sorry, I thought you would still be cooking for us."

"Why would I do that?" Brittany asked. "I don't want to work all day, then come home and cook all night. One job is enough, thank you very much."

"Okay, okay. I'll do the cooking from now on! I just...I dunno, I just didn't think about making dinner tonight. I was too distracted."

"Well, that's fair. I'd be distracted if *I* got interrogated by the police." Brittany rubbed the side of her neck. "So what do you want for dinner?"

"Pizza."

"Ew, no. I know we've got some chicken in the fridge. You could add seasoning, and—"

"Too late, I already picked pizza!" I said quickly. "I'm the stay-at-home parent, so I get to decide. Besides, I haven't seen Scott in a while."

"All right, just as long as you get it quick. I'm starving."

The pizza place is about five minutes away from our house. My friend Scott works there. He's actually the manager, believe it or not. The two of us started working there in high school. I quit once I went off to college, but he stuck with it while he was getting his degree in Computer Engineering. He was planning to use his degree to get a job in the tech industry, but he got promoted to assistant manager of the store, so he decided to stay with pizza making instead. Fast-forward to today, and now he's the full manager. I guess it all worked out for him, but I couldn't imagine running a pizza store myself.

Scott was working the front counter when I arrived. He was wearing the standard uniform for his store: a black hat and a green shirt with pizza slices on them. I don't think I've seen him wear anything other than that uniform for the past five years.

As usual, he gave me the employee discount. I'll be honest: that's the main reason I love going to his pizza place. The pizza's pretty good, too.

"Shouldn't be more than ten minutes," Scott said. "It's a slow night. I had to send one of the delivery drivers home. So, what's up with you?"

"Not much," I said. "I just started watching the baby full-time, and—"

Scott's eyebrows shot up and disappeared under the brim of his hat. "Whoa, you were *serious* about that? I saw you posted that on social media, but I thought you were joking!"

"No joke. I'm a stay-at-home dad now."

"Wow. Better you than me, dude. You carry a purse around all the time now?"

"It's called a diaper bag."

43

"No, it's called a purse," Scott said knowingly. "You sure you can handle watching the baby all the time? It's a lot of work."

"Yes, I'm sure I can handle it," I said, a little annoyed. "Why do people keep asking me that? I'm great at watching my kid."

"Dude, I saw your dorm room in college. You're a total slob who can't cook."

"That's *everyone's* dorm room in college," I said. "I'm way more responsible now, and besides, I'm a great cook."

"Then why are you getting dinner at a pizza place?"

"...Fair point. I'll pick up a recipe book from the library, or something." I normally cooked lunch for Brittany and me on the weekends. Going from cooking once or twice a week to cooking every day couldn't be *that* bad, could it? "You wanna know the worst part about being a stay-at-home dad?"

"Everyone thinks you're a creepy weirdo?"

"Uh, no." I hope that's not what people thought about me. Although based on the way the moms at baby playtime reacted to me, maybe he was right. "I was going to say the front pack. It's like wearing a corset with shoulder straps. My back still hurts from using it this morning."

"That's rough. So, where's the baby now? Is your wife watching her?"

"Of course. I wouldn't leave the kid in the car while I went in to get pizza. I'm not *that* bad at parenting."

"You'd be surprised at some of the crazy stuff I've seen. About a month ago, this one kid—"

"*Hiii* Scott," a voice said.

\* \* \*

*Suspect Dossier*

Name: Deirdre Simmons

Occupation: Hair stylist

Alternate Occupation: Online book reviewer, just like me. She mostly reviews books from the *Francy Droo* series. I guess you could say we're kind of rivals.

Number of Followers: Way more than I have, unfortunately.

Physical Description: Short black hair, almost always has a hair clip on the left side of her head. I have no idea why. Often wears short skirts to show off her legs.

Marital Status: Single, obviously. At least, obvious to *me*. She's not very—I mean to say that—okay, the two of us dated each other for about a month in high school, but that was before I met Brittany. We broke up *because* I met Brittany, in fact. It's a long story, and I don't want to get into it right now.

Motive for Murder: She might be snarky, but that doesn't make her a killer. At least, I *hope* she's not a killer, because I'd probably be on her list of potential victims.

* * *

Scott's eyes went goopier than his triple-cheese pizza as he looked at her. "Hi, Deirdre. What would you like to order?"

"Three extra-large pizzas. One cheese, one pepperoni, one combo," she said.

"That's a lot of pizza for one person," I noted.

Deirdre scowled at me. "The pizza's not for me. It's for the Mystery Club. We're meeting at the library this week."

"Mystery Club, huh? What, you guys read mystery books or something?"

"That's exactly what we do." She brushed some invisible dirt off of her shoulder. "Only we read *real* mysteries, not the Harvey Brothers garbage. You should come. You'd probably like it."

"Can't. Too busy."

Deirdre fake-smiled at me. "It must be difficult when your wife never lets you go anywhere."

I scowled back at Deirdre. "It's not my wife. It's my baby. I have to watch her."

"Oh, yeah, I heard you were watching her all the time now. How funny is that? You're a house husband! Who knew?"

"Why is that funny?" I asked angrily.

"You don't have any brothers or sisters," Deirdre said. "Did you ever baby-sit when you were growing up?"

"No."

"And that's what I'm saying. This is your *first time* watching a kid."

"Yeah, but it's *my* kid," I said defensively. "That makes a difference."

"For her sake, I hope you're right, or you'll be the guy whose kid screams in the grocery store all the time. What was her name again? Miss Coffee?"

"McKenzie."

"Cute. Not as good as *Deirdre*, but still cute. Well, if you ever need a baby-sitter, I'm sure you can ask...Scott."

"I don't watch babies," Scott protested.

"Sad," Deirdre said. "You might get more customers that way." She slid her credit card through the machine and marched straight for the bathroom, dangling her keys in front of her. "*Byeee*, Scott. Make the pizza extra-yummy for me!"

Scott watched her leave.

"You think she's into me?" he asked hopefully.

I looked him over. Scott was a nice guy, but he samples too much of his pizza, if you know what I mean. Plus, I can't picture a hair stylist going out with a guy who wears a hat all the time.

"Not a chance," I said. "I'm pretty sure she would never want to be seen with someone whose clothes have permanent tomato sauce stains."

"Shoot."

* * *

*"Finally,"* Brittany said, as I came in with the pizza. "Give it to me." She took the pizza box from my hands and pulled out a slice.

"Whoa! Aren't we going to eat at the table?" I asked.

"We *would*, but you made a mess." She pointed to the kitchen table, where I had put McKenzie's diapers.

"Sorry," I said. "I meant to throw them away, but I forgot."

"Just remember to throw out the diaper as soon as you change the baby, and you'll be fine," Brittany said. She took a big bite out of her pizza slice. "Don't forget the folding technique, either."

I grimaced. Brittany has a magical diaper-folding technique, where she folds them so tightly, they're about the size of a dollar bill. She's tried teaching me how to do it at least four times already, but I just can't seem to get it right. Whenever I try folding diapers, they end up looking more like baseballs.

I carried the diapers to the outside trash can, as she put McKenzie in her playpen. The two of us talked some more as we ate the pizza. She brought me up to speed on all the people at her work, which was interesting, although nowhere near as interesting as a murder investigation. After that, we started talking about the baby playtime group.

"You didn't tell me it was a mom's group," I said.

"It's not. It's a baby playtime group," Brittany said.

"Yeah, but all the other people there are *moms*. I was the only dad there."

"Lucky you," Brittany smiled.

I shook my head. She didn't seem to understand how difficult it was to be the only stay-at-home dad in town. I had really been counting on having other dads to help me out. "No, not lucky. It was awkward. They acted like I didn't belong with them."

"They're just not used to seeing McKenzie with anyone else besides me. They'll need some time to warm up to you."

47

"Yeah, like five years. Workout Mom kept criticizing me for doing everything wrong."

"Workout Mom? You mean Sara?"

"Probably. I don't remember any of their names except the Jennifers."

"Don't worry. You'll learn all their names soon enough. If you go every day, I'm sure you'll be chatting like old friends by the end of the week."

"But I *already* talked to them! I mean, I *tried* talking to them. It was awkward. They talked about getting pregnant, which I totally didn't want to know about, thank you very much, and they all looked at me like I was crazy when I told them the story of how you threw the pregnancy test at my head."

"What? You moron! Why would you do that?" She picked up a napkin and threw it at my head. Then she started giggling like an idiot.

"Very funny," I muttered.

"I thought it was," she said, smiling. That's part of the reason we make such a great couple: we both think our silly little jokes are hilarious. "So you felt a little awkward around the moms at first. That's not so bad."

"Yeah, but it happened *the whole time!* I sang the songs wrong, I didn't know the hand motions, and when we did the parachute thing, I smashed into the really hot—I mean, the tall one. The one that looks like a movie star."

Brittany gave me a serious look. "*Please* don't tell me you're crushing on one of my mom friends."

"I'm not!" I protested. "I'm just saying, she's incredibly—" I was going to say "attractive", but I realized that was not a good way to end that sentence. "...skinny?"

"So, you *are* attracted to her."

I choked on my pizza. "Uh..."

"Ned, you need to stay away from her. I'm serious. I trust you, but she's a man-stealer. She's cheated on every man she's ever been with."

48

Whoa. I didn't know baby playtime group came with juicy gossip.

"Really?"

"Yes," Brittany said. She folded her arms against her chest. "I've even seen her in action. She will flirt with *any* man, whether he's married or not. Do yourself a favor and stay away from that blonde monster."

"Blonde? I was talking about the redhead. The tall one with the foreign name?"

"*Oh.*" She let out a huge sigh of relief. "She's okay. I like her. I thought you meant Jessica Wakeford."

"Never heard of her."

"Good. Keep it that way. I don't like to say bad things about other people, but...she's a disaster waiting to happen."

"You know I would never cheat on you. I love you too much."

"I love you, too." She paused for a moment. "So you think the redhead is hot, do you?"

"I refuse to answer that question."

"Because I was thinking of dyeing my hair red, just to see what it'd be like..."

My heart started beating faster at the thought of my wife with red hair, but I tried to ignore it. "You're just teasing me."

"And since you like tall women, I was going to start wearing platform shoes all the time. Eventually, I'd switch to stilts, but I have to start small."

"Stop joking about this."

"And I have to change my name to something foreign and exotic. Something like Brittanoshkiafumph."

"Ha ha, we get it!" I exclaimed sarcastically. "The joke is over! Can we *please* stop talking about this?"

"You're too fun to tease sometimes," she said. "Good thing I trust the other moms, or I'd be worried about one of them trying to steal you away."

## Chapter 6

*"Fred, take a look at this," Jim said. "The cottage is a mess!"*

*"Someone must have been searching through it," Fred said, looking at the upended mattress and piles of clothes everywhere. "Wonder what they were looking for?"*

*"Or, maybe someone was trying to leave here in a hurry. Either way, we have to figure out who this cottage belongs to."*

*"That's simple enough. We just—"*

"Waaah!"

*"—at the—"*

"—Aaa!"

*"—and—"*

"Aaa aaa aaaaa!"

I put my *Harvey Brothers* book down. "Okay, McKenzie, I hear you! I'm coming!"

You'd think watching a three-month-old would give me plenty of free time for reading. I mean, she can't even crawl yet. But no, if I left her alone for too long she would let me know it. It felt like I was busy every single hour of the day, even though I didn't do much besides change diapers and feed the baby.

I pulled out my phone to check the time. It was about an hour before baby playtime. Yes, I was going back to the baby playtime group. Sure, it made me feel stupid and awkward, but it was an excuse to go outside and do something. Your options are pretty limited when you've got an infant.

Plus, my curiosity was piqued by what my wife had said last night. Brittany almost *never* says bad things about other people. She was even on good terms with Deirdre Simmons, the few times they had been together. So, if Jessica Wakeford was bad enough to get my wife upset, then she had to be legitimately awful.

Before I put my phone back, I noticed an email from the website I posted my videos to. Odd. They normally never emailed me, unless there was a problem. Curious, I opened it up to see what was going on.

It *was* a problem. One of my videos had been flagged as "inappropriate content", so they demonetized it, which meant no advertisements would play before the video. In other words, I wouldn't get any money from it anymore.

"There has to be a mistake somewhere," I said. I reread the email, but nope, I read it correctly the first time. What video had they demonetized?

It was my review for the first book in the *Harvey Brothers Mystery Adventures* series. I let out a low curse. The first video in a series is always the one that gets the most views. *Always.* Why had they demonetized one of my most popular videos? Why couldn't they have demonetized one of the videos no one watched, instead?

I wondered if there was a way to appeal the decision. My videos weren't inappropriate content! But then again, what counted as "inappropriate content"? I *was* reviewing a book with a kidnapping. Maybe some people would consider that to be inappropriate. I could understand that, but still. We're talking about a children's book. It didn't have any profanity or violence. I would be totally fine with McKenzie reading it when she got older.

I searched for more information, hoping to see if anyone else had problems with this. No luck. It looked like it was just me. Well, wasn't that great? I tried to figure out what *specifically* made the video inappropriate, but I couldn't find that either. It was almost like I needed the Harvey Brothers to solve this mystery.

*"Fred, I can't figure out what's wrong with the video," Jim said.*

*"I think the problem is that he gave the book a three out of ten," Fred said. "It deserves a way higher score."*

*"You think the culprit could be an angry ghostwriter, out for revenge?"*

*"Either that, or a—"*

"Waaah aaa aaaaa!"

"Sorry! Sorry!" I said, as I put down the phone and went to the baby. She seemed hungry, so I made a bottle of formula. After two days, I was getting a lot better at not spilling it all over the counter. I shook it all up, when I noticed the time.

"Oh, geez, no time for feeding, we're gonna be late for baby playtime! Sorry! Daddy didn't mean to spend the morning on the phone!"

I cursed myself for being a bad parent, and I wondered if I should just skip baby playtime altogether. Formula only stays good for about an hour. After that, you have to dump it, so I didn't have much time to feed McKenzie before the formula went bad.

That's when I got a great idea. I would take her in the stroller. That way, I could feed her and walk her at the same time. It would solve both problems, and best of all, I wouldn't have to mess with the front pack!

I put the bottle of formula in the diaper bag and took McKenzie to the car. We keep the stroller inside the car trunk, because it's too big to leave it in our house all the time. It's actually a combination stroller and car seat. I put her inside the car seat, and I lowered it into the stroller like I had seen my wife do.

I paused.

It didn't click. It was supposed to make a clicking noise, right? Why didn't it click?

I pushed the seat back and forth. Yep, it was loose.

I picked it up and tried turning it around the other way. Nope. I tried pushing down as hard as I could, while twisting it, and...

*Click.*

Great, it was in place now. I grabbed the handle to make sure, and—uh oh. Only the left side was in place. The right side was still loose.

I sighed. "Come on, McKenzie, let's just drive to playtime today."

* * *

When I got to baby playtime, the doorway was blocked by two people, who were openly making out. I wasn't able to get a good look at them, because they were facing each other, but I figured this was the infamous Jessica. She had a heavy tan, blonde hair that fell to her shoulders, ripped jeans and a cutoff shirt that said "world's" something on it. Maybe "world's best mom", although that was debatable, since I didn't see her child with her anywhere. The guy had a flannel shirt, brown hair that was longer than hers, and he was at least ten years younger than her. Gross.

I waited a few seconds for them to move, but it soon became obvious that they weren't paying attention to anyone other than each other.

"Can you take that somewhere else?" I asked.

The woman stopped kissing long enough to shoot me a dirty look, then went back to making out. I could see why my wife didn't like her.

"Seriously, making out in a doorway is a fire hazard. Could you please move?"

"Bite me," the guy said. He flipped his hair over his shoulder and rolled his head in around. He probably thought that made him look intimidating, but in reality, it looked more like he was imitating a bobblehead doll.

I began to wish I *had* brought the stroller after all. That way, I could run over their feet. I was forced to squeeze past them to get inside. The diaper bag smashed uncomfortably against my hip, but I was able to make it through without hurting McKenzie.

I stumbled into the room, rubbing my hip. Who knew there would be a physical challenge just to get into baby playtime?

"Oh. You're back," said Workout Mom. She was wearing hot pink workout clothes today. "How nice."

"Are those the same clothes you had on yesterday?" Crazy Hair asked.

"Uh...I'm not sure," I said. I couldn't remember, to be honest. The previous day had been a blur of police interrogations and dirty diapers. Oh, and pizza. I remembered having pizza. It was delicious.

I looked at my shirt, which had a cartoon superhero on it. I'm pretty sure large cartoon characters are part of the official stay-at-home dad uniform. I saw some baby spit-up on my shoulder, and I sniffed it discreetly. Yep, that was at least a day old. I shrugged apologetically. "Sorry, I didn't have time to change."

"At least your baby is wearing something different," Crazy Hair muttered. She moved to the side of the room across from me.

McKenzie *was* wearing something different, but I couldn't take credit for that. Brittany had changed her into bedtime clothes the previous night. I, uh...hadn't changed her out of them. I made a mental note to step up my stay-at-home dad game, or at least, to do a better job of hiding my incompetence in front of the other parents.

Gosh, maybe my friends were right. Maybe I *wasn't* cut out to be a stay-at-home dad.

Nah, that wasn't right. I just wasn't used to it yet. After all, this was only my second day on the job. At least, I thought it was. Was it my third? I had lost count. Today was Thursday, right? No, that couldn't be it. Monday was when Mr. O'Neill was killed, and that had been the day before yesterday, so...

"Wednesday!" I said. "It's Wednesday."

"We aren't singing the days of the week song yet," Workout Mom said.

"Sorry, long day," I said. I pulled out the bottle of formula and started feeding McKenzie, so I would have an excuse not to talk to anyone.

The group was mostly the same as the day before. Crazy Hair had put the left side of her head in a braid, which actually looked kind of nice, but it was too late for me to change her nickname from Crazy Hair to something else. She was sitting with someone who looked like her sister. Her long hair was tousled and hung over her shoulders, almost like her shoulders were cold, and she wanted to keep them warm.

The Jennifers were missing, and in their place was a grandmother I didn't know. Not that I'm on a first-name basis with all the grandmothers in town, but you know what I mean. Movie Star Mom was wearing an all-blue jogging suit, and she was showing off her new purse to everyone else. They gushed over it, and said how lucky she was to have one. Me, I had no idea what the big deal was. A purse is a purse, in my opinion. It *did* look expensive, though. Maybe that's what had everyone so impressed.

I looked at my purple diaper bag. Maybe if I put my name on it with pink sequins, people would be impressed by it, too.

Once again, I was next to Sleeping Woman. She was already sitting down, asleep. I found it a little weird that she was sleeping through baby playtime again. I mean, I could understand not getting enough sleep with a baby in the house, but this is not exactly the best time to catch up on naps. There's too much talking going on.

We got started at eleven o'clock, with the *Hello Babies* song. The lyrics are:

*Hello babies*
*Hello babies*
*Hello babies*
*Hello hello*

Come to think of it, that's basically the same as the *Goodbye Babies* song. Actually, most of the songs at baby playtime have the same tune, with different lyrics. Either Workout Mom didn't know many songs, or she just didn't bother with being creative. It's not like the babies would notice.

I'm proud to say I remembered all the hand signals for *Hello Babies*; although to be fair, it's only one hand signal, and it's waving hello, so it's not that big of an accomplishment, and I don't care! Just let me have this minor success, okay?

I hadn't seen Jessica since I walked past her in the doorway. She came in halfway through the song. And I mean *halfway*. She stomped in, sat down and started talking, like we weren't already in the middle of something. Now that I could see her shirt, I saw that it read "World's Hottest Hottie", which kind of made no sense.

"Ugh, guys!" Jessica said, rolling her eyes. "I don't know why Todd is so jealous of Bruce!"

"Hello, Jessica," Workout Mom said. "Are you ready to help— ?"

56

But Jessica already had her phone out, and she was playing with it. "Ugh, no. You do your baby thing. I gotta email Jeffrey about our date tonight. I need to cancel, because I already made plans with Ken."

I scratched my head. Was...was she dating four guys at the same time?

"Is Ken your husband or boyfriend?" I asked politely.

Jessica laughed herself sick. "No way! You're thinking of Bruce the Baby Daddy. I'd never *marry* anyone, though, because it's just a—hey! Why is there a *guy* here? This group is supposed to be girls only!"

"Baby playtime is open to everyone," Workout Mom said.

"I—" I began to say.

"Whatever," Jessica said. "I'm outta here. Later." She put her toddler down, took a selfie, then left the room.

"Is...is she always like that?" I asked the group.

"Yes," said Movie Star Mom.

"Totally," said the grandmother.

"She always drops off her baby at the start, then comes back to pick him up an hour later," Workout Mom said. She put her hands on her hips angrily. "I've *told* her this isn't a daycare, and she has to stay the whole time, but she doesn't care."

Crazy Hair had the last word on the subject. "At least she didn't try hitting on you."

"That is *definitely* a good thing," I agreed. I had no interest in becoming Boyfriend #5.

It took about ten minutes, before Jessica's toddler noticed me. He stood up and walked right towards me, stopping about six inches from my face.

"Uh, hi," I said.

He stared at me angrily. His uncombed blonde hair fell down the side of his head, and his eyebrows furrowed into his large eyes.

"Nice to meet you?" I asked.

His frown got deeper, and I started to feel a little unnerved.

"You're going to be a bouncer when you grow up, aren't you?"

He leaned closer to me.

"Okay, yeah, that's enough." I picked him up by his overalls and turned him around, but he turned right back around and got closer to me. This kid was seriously invading my personal bubble. Not cool. And I couldn't complain about it to his mother, because she wasn't there.

"Aw, he likes you," Movie Star Mom said.

"Uh, more like he's challenging me for dominance." The kid was acting like we were lions, and he was in a fight to the death, for control of the herd.

That's when he punched me.

"Ow!" I yelped. I picked him up, walked him to the other side of the room, and then set him down. By the time I got back to my seat, he was already back, standing between me and McKenzie, looking at me like, "Your daughter belongs to *me* now. Whatcha gonna do about it, loser?"

Would it be like this when McKenzie became a teenager? I sincerely hoped not.

I reached around him and picked up McKenzie, placing her securely on my lap.

The angry toddler shouted, "GAH!" at me before turning around and storming off. Disaster averted...only for a little bit, though. On the other side of the room, he started picking fights with the other kids. As in, he pushed a girl out of his way and stole her toy. When she tried to take it back, he hit her with it.

"That is *not okay*," Workout Mom said, pushing the angry boy aside. "We *do not hit* other people." He bit her. "You little monster!"

He ignored her and started hitting the baby girl again. She screamed.

"Stop him, Ned!" Workout Mom said.

"What? Why me?" I asked.

"You're the only one he pays attention to!"

"Uh, okay," I muttered. I went across the room, and sure enough, he stopped to stare at me. How do you scold a toddler? It seems kind of pointless to me. It's not like they can understand any of the words you're saying. I pretended he *could* speak fluent English and said, "You should behave better. Got it?"

He closed his eyes and grunted several times. What was he doing? That was strange.

Then the smell hit me. "Did you just poop? I think he just pooped!"

"So change him," Crazy Hair said.

"I'm pretty sure I don't have diapers in his size," I said.

"I can do it," Crazy Hair's sister volunteered. That's when I decided I liked her.

We had six or so minutes of peace, until they came back. Jessica's baby toddled straight towards me again, like a baby on a mission.

"Da ba baba," he said.

"Da ba baba yourself," I told him.

He stared angrily at me.

I stared back at him, until he took a step backwards and began crying. Victory!

"Why'd you make him cry?" Crazy Hair asked. "*What did you do to him?*"

"Nothing!" I said. "I just looked at him, that's all!"

"You shouldn't be mean to toddlers," Workout Mom said.

I started to say, "He was being mean to me first!", but luckily, I realized how pathetic it sounded for me to complain about a small child bullying me.

"Sorry," I said. "It was an accident. He was acting weird."

"He *is* Jessica's son," Crazy Hair said. "That's to be expected."

"Maybe he thinks you're his new dad," Movie Star Mom suggested.

"Uh, no," I said. "That's not happening."

I picked up the grumpy toddler and put him in front of Sleeping Woman. She didn't wake up or move. He looked at her for a few moments, then glanced at me, then went back to looking at her. He tried crawling over her leg to get to me, but she started grunting. Startled, he backed away.

Excellent. She made a natural playpen.

He seemed too scared to disturb Sleeping Woman, so he sat quietly between her legs for the rest of the meeting. The only other problem he caused was when he tried to throw his shoe at me, but I was able to catch it before it hit me.

Compared to the wild child, the rest of baby playtime was great. All of the other babies were well-behaved, and McKenzie loved the game where I lifted her up into the air. If it was that nice all the time, I could see why my wife took the baby here so often.

Still, I didn't want to risk any more problems with Jessica's son, so I decided to leave when the singing portion of the playtime group was over. Maybe someday I'd stay for an extra half-hour to chat with the other parents while the babies played.

As I left the building, I saw Jessica making out with some guy in the hallway. And I'm pretty sure it wasn't the same guy she was kissing earlier. I did her a favor and brought out her toddler. He toddled straight to her and grabbed her legs, breaking up the kissing session.

I smiled and waved at her. She did not seem happy with me, but I had a feeling my wife would be proud of me.

I was feeling good after leaving baby playtime, until I checked my phone when I reached the car. I had another email, saying one of my videos was demonetized. Two in the same day? One might be a glitch in the system, but two was a pattern.

Someone had done this on purpose.

# Chapter 7

My suspicions were confirmed when I saw that the video was my review of the second book in the *Harvey Brothers Mystery Adventures* series. Both the first and second book of the series were flagged as inappropriate? That couldn't be a coincidence. That series has been running for decades with over a hundred books in it. I hadn't reviewed all of them yet, but the odds of a computer picking two books at random, and having them be the first two books, were something like one in ten thousand.

I know it sounds a little silly to be worrying about two videos getting demonetized, especially when neither video makes more than a quarter per month, but now that I was no longer an accountant, online reviews were my main money-making business. Besides, at the rate my videos were being flagged, all of my videos would get hit soon.

More importantly, though, my phone had a voicemail from my old work.

"Hi, Ned. It's Kelly. I know you came by the office yesterday, but I'm gonna need you to come back. We found your credit card in your cubicle, and I'm sure you'd rather get that in person than have us mail it to you. Plus, we have...stuff to talk about."

Sweet, the credit card trick worked, although I didn't like the sound of the "stuff" she wanted to talk about. That sounded a little ominous, considering the murder investigation and all. For a brief moment, I wondered if I was making a mistake investigating.

I mean, I knew I was innocent. I should trust the police officers to do their jobs to prove it. By looking into the crime on my own, I ran the risk of interfering with the investigation and causing a lot of problems for myself. On the other hand, I might speed the investigation along by finding some good evidence.

I thought about it for a few moments, before deciding to continue. I was just going to talk to some of my former co-workers. That wasn't interfering with a police investigation. That was just being a normal person. Right?

Plus, if my online followers found out I had the chance to solve a real-life murder mystery and had done nothing, they would never have forgiven me. Nope! I would have to make the Harvey Brothers proud and solve *The Mystery of the Murdered Boss*. Was that the right name for this mystery? Maybe *The Secret of Mr. O'Neill*. What if he didn't have a secret, though? Then the name wouldn't fit. Maybe *Murder at the Office*. No, *Office Murder*. Maybe something comical, like *Who Killed the Boss?*

That's why I read mysteries instead of writing them. It's too difficult.

McKenzie must have been tired after baby playtime, because she fell asleep in the car as I drove to work. I replied to Kelly's text message, then I changed McKenzie's diaper in the front seat. By the time I got inside the building, Kelly was there for me in the waiting area. We sat together in some green chairs by the main doors, about ten feet away from Barry's security desk.

McKenzie was in her car seat. One of her burp cloths was in her hand, and she flapped it around a bit. She wasn't making any noise, and she didn't seem interested in me or Kelly. Kelly was wearing a suit jacket with matching pants and a freshly-ironed shirt. Her hair was pulled back, except for a strand in the front which hung down over her forehead. There was a shiny gold card sticking out of her pocket.

"Hi," I said. I pointed at the card. "What's that?"

"I got promoted to fill Mr. O'Neill's position," she said. "This is my temporary ID card. The official one comes in next week."

"Congratulations. Does this mean you'll be getting his old office?" A week ago, I might have been jealous, but now? You couldn't pay me enough to work there. I could *never* picture myself working in an office where someone had been killed.

"Yes, as soon as the police open it up again. I'm going to get rid of everything in there, first. It doesn't seem right to keep Mr. O'Neill's things."

"I agree. I'm told you have my credit card?"

She pulled it out of her pocket and handed it to me. "Here it is. Cute trick."

"Trick? What do you mean?"

"Pretending to drop your credit card, so you'd have an excuse to come back here." Kelly glared at me. "There is literally no other reason why you'd pull out your credit card while working at your cubicle."

"Maybe I was making some online purchases."

"Not on company computers, you weren't!" she snapped. "That's against office policy!"

"Yes, well, murder is against office policy, but that didn't stop our culprit," I pointed out. "Are there any new leads in the case?"

Kelly sighed. "I have no idea who the killer could be. I don't think *you* did it. I don't think *anyone* did it. I trust everyone in the office."

"Do you think the killer could be an outsider, then?"

"I don't know what to think. This is all so hectic. I've had to field over ten of Mr. O'Neill's calls these last couple of days. I barely have time to think. I just wish the police would catch the killer, soon."

"Me, too," I said. "Did you see anything suspicious that day?"

Lucky for me, Kelly was a cooperative witness, and she didn't object to my questions. I guess she was used to talking to other people about the murder.

"Besides you being led off by security? No," she said. "After you left, it was totally quiet. I didn't hear any noise from Mr. O'Neill's office, and the only time I saw someone leave their cubicle was when Alan went to the bathroom."

I thought about that for a moment. Mr. O'Neill's office—and Kelly's desk, by extension—was purposely located at the end of the aisle of cubicles. That way, he could look out of the office and see everyone who's on our team.

"Did you only look in the direction of the cubicles?"

"Yes. That's the direction my desk faces. You know that. There's no reason for me to turn around and look at the wall."

"Hm..." The office next to Mr. O'Neill's belonged to one of the vice presidents, and the office beyond that one belonged to the CFO. "So someone could have come from the direction of the other offices, without you seeing them."

Kelly shook her head. "I don't think that's possible. It doesn't matter what direction the killer came from. If someone opened the door to Mr. O'Neill's office, I would have heard them."

It *was* unlikely that someone could open the door to Mr. O'Neill's office five feet from behind Kelly without her hearing a thing. Plus, O'Neill liked to shout whenever someone interrupted him. Either the killer was amazingly quiet, or O'Neill was expecting the murderer to show up. But was it possible that Kelly was distracted at one point?

"Did you listen to music at all?"

"No. That's against the rules."

"Did you take a phone call, or something else that involved noise?"

"I had a call at four, but that was just me making plans for dinner. It didn't take more than three minutes, I'd bet."

I had to grin at that, because Kelly had once chewed me out for calling my wife, while at work. "Making a personal call on company time? Isn't that against the rules?"

"You watch your mouth, Mister Gray!" she snapped. "I'll have you know, I went on break before making that call. You can check my timesheet if you don't believe me!"

"I don't need to see your timesheet," I said. "When was your break?"

"Four to four-thirty, and before you ask, yes. I left the building after I made the phone call."

I glanced at Barry on the other side of the room. It looked like he was reading something, and not paying any attention to us.

"When was Barry's break?" I asked.

"Four-fifteen to four-thirty."

"The same time as yours?!"

"I don't sync my break schedule with the security guard, but I know what you're thinking. There was a fifteen-minute gap when someone easily could have entered Mr. O'Neill's office and killed him." She was right, and that was good news for me. I was long gone, by the time 4:00 p.m. had rolled around. If the autopsy proved the murder happened then, my innocence would be assured.

"Did anyone see you during your break?"

"Nope. I don't think anybody saw Barry, either. At least, that's what he said."

So, neither of them had alibis for the time in question. That made things trickier.

"Did you notice anything different when you returned to your desk?"

"Nope. Everything was the same."

"Can I see it?"

Kelly glared at me again. "No way. Mr. O'Neill's office is a police *crime scene*, and besides, you're not allowed to be in the building as a partial employee."

I was talking about seeing her desk, not the crime scene, but I suppose it didn't matter. "Partial employee? What does that mean?"

"It means you're not a full employee, but you're not an ex-employee yet," she said. "Which is part of the reason why I needed you to come here. You have to sign the release form. I printed out another copy."

Kelly handed me a folder with a paper inside. I checked to make sure McKenzie was still doing okay, and then quickly scanned the document.

It seemed like a standard resignation letter. It said I was leaving the company willingly, and that I wasn't going to give away any company secrets, that sort of thing. At the bottom of the page were two lines. I was supposed to sign on the line at the bottom/right, but I didn't have a pen. I was going to ask for one, when I noticed the line on the bottom/left already had a signature.

"You signed this?" I asked.

"Since I'm the acting manager, yes," Kelly said.

"Is this the document that went missing?"

Kelly sat up straighter in her chair. "How do you know about that?"

"Detective Dodd mentioned something about it," I said vaguely, hoping she could supply me with more details.

"Yes, this is the document that went missing. As you can see, it's a standard form. All you have to do is switch out the employee's name and the manager's name. The manager has to sign it before the employee does, though. It's one of the rules. I was going to email it to you, once Mr. O'Neill signed it and gave it back to me."

"He didn't do it?"

"Obviously not. I figured he was busy."

Either that, or he was dead by the time she sent him the form. "When was this?" I asked.

"Right after you left. Mr. O'Neill had sent me a copy of the form last week, so I had it all ready to go on my computer."

Now *that* was interesting. Why did Mr. O'Neill prepare a resignation form the week before? Had he been planning on firing someone? He *did* say the company was having financial problems...

"And the police didn't find the paperwork in his office?"

"That's what they said. Unless his printer was out of ink, I have no idea why that would be the case. I *definitely* printed it out on his printer."

There are three printers that everyone in our group has access to: Mr. O'Neill's, Kelly's, and the general printer that everyone else has to share. The computers are set to print on Mr. O'Neill's printer, by default. It's kind of a pain, because we have to manually select the group printer every single time we use it.

I gave the folder back to Kelly. "This looks good to me. Do you have a pen for me to sign with? I don't carry one in my diaper bag."

"Sure, follow me inside."

Great! I would get a chance to check out her desk! Sure, I had seen it dozens of times before, but not when trying to determine how the culprit could have sneaked past her without being heard. I picked up McKenzie— she groaned a little, but she didn't make any other noises—and I followed Kelly further into the building. I was excited for about thirty seconds, until I realized she was leading me into the supply room.

"Oh," I said.

"Something wrong?" Kelly asked.

"No." Maybe I could learn something useful in the supply room. Slyly, I asked, "Are the three-hole punch machines still stored in the cabinet?"

"Third drawer from the top, right-hand side."

I tried pulling open the drawer, but it was stuck.

"You can only open one drawer at a time with that cabinet."

"Right. I knew that." I pushed the top drawer closed and opened the drawer I wanted. Inside, I found...four three-hole punch machines. They looked perfectly normal. No clues there.

"Happy with your investigation, Sherlock?" I turned around to find Kelly smirking at me. Oops. She knew what I was doing the whole time. I guess I wasn't as sneaky as I thought.

"I'm more like Fred Harvey, but yeah. These don't look like they've been touched for a while." The two in the back of the drawer had some dust on them, but the two in the front didn't. I guess when people borrowed a three-hole punch, they just took whatever was in the front of the drawer. "Did the police fingerprint these?"

"Nope. There was no need to. The three-hole punch that killed Mr. O'Neill was on the ground next to him."

"How did they know it was the murder weapon?" I asked.

"It was covered in blood," she said, shuddering slightly. "It was awful."

"So, you *saw* the crime scene? What did you—?"

"I don't want to talk about it. It was...it was awful. I'm going to leave it at that. Here's your pen."

Kelly looked upset, so I decided not to push her. I signed the document and gave her back the pen. "Is that all you need?"

"Just about. You've got nine and a half vacation days left. Do you want me to cash them out and add the money to your final paycheck?"

"Sure, sounds good to me," I said. "Anything else?"

"No, that should be it. I told the IT people to delete you from the system. They said it should take about a week. If they run into any problems, I'll let you know."

That was when Alan stumbled into the room. I highly doubted this was a coincidence; he probably saw me and decided to come over. I thought *I* was the worst-dressed person in the office with shorts and a t-shirt, but no. Alan's brightly-colored shirt clashed horribly with his tie, which was louder than he was.

"Well, if it isn't Wonderful Wednesday!" he exclaimed. "What are you doing here, Ned? Haven't been buried under a pile of diapers yet? And Kelly! Our new manager! I didn't know the stock room was an office party, ha! Why do they call it a stock room, anyway? It's not like we sell stocks here."

"Can I help you with something?" Kelly asked, in a polite voice with just a twinge of annoyance.

"I just need a three-hole punch," Alan said. I stepped aside so he could get at the drawer. He waggled his fingers in the air, then grabbed a dusty one from the back of the drawer.

"Do you always use that three-hole punch?" I asked.

"Oh, every day!" he said. "I dress it up in a wig and call it Sally! Ha! You kill me with these jokes, Ned! As long as you don't kill me with a three-hole punch. That'd be awful."

"You shouldn't make jokes about that," said Kelly, offended.

*You shouldn't make jokes, period*, I thought to myself.

"Okay, okay!" He put the three-hole punch on the counter and inserted a group of about ten pages. The paper on top kept flipping up at the end, and he struggled to get it inside. "Stupid thing! How do you make it work?"

"Maybe you should punch the papers in two groups, instead of doing them all at once," I suggested.

"Oh. Right." Alan took out the top half of his pile, then pushed the handle backwards. He grunted and pushed it harder. "It's not working!"

I tried to resist the urge to groan. "You need to push *down* on the handle."

"Oh. Right!" He pushed down on the handle with all his might, and accidentally knocked the three-hole punch on the ground. Alan's comedy of errors made me glad I wasn't working in an office any more. Not dealing with incompetent co-workers is a major benefit of being a stay-at-home dad. How did Alan manage to keep his job?

"Yesterday, I thought you said you used three-hole punches all the time," I said.

Alan looked ashamed of himself. "I was just bragging to look cool."

"What's so cool about using basic office equipment?" Kelly asked.

"Well, it's not cool if you *can't*," Alan said. That was an understatement. "I also have problems with closing binders on my fingers. Those things *hurt!* Maybe you could help me?"

"Maybe, if you answer a few questions," I replied. "Where were you yesterday afternoon?"

Alan's eyes bulged out, and he dropped the three-hole punch on his foot and let out a cry. "Ouch! That hurts!" McKenzie squealed at him. "I...I was sitting at my desk, I swear! I didn't kill Mr. O'Neill! Kelly will tell you, won't you, Kelly?"

"I didn't see him leave his cubicle," Kelly said.

"Right!" Alan said. "I'm totally innocent. The only thing I'm guilty of is being attractive!"

I groaned, even though I made the same basic joke the day before. What can I say? The joke was a lot funnier when *I* said it. "Did you go on break at any time?" I asked.

"Four fifteen," he said.

"Does *everyone* go on break at four fifteen?" I certainly never took a break that close to leaving the office.

"That's the latest you can take a break," Kelly explained. "A few years ago, we had problems with people not taking their breaks, then trying to leave the office early. So it was decided that if you *don't* take your fifteen-minute break by four fifteen, you don't get one. Those are the rules."

I had never heard of that rule, but I figured Kelly knew what she was talking about. Still, it was way too much of a coincidence that everyone was gone, without an alibi, at the exact same time.

"I sometimes end up working through my break by accident," Alan said. "That's because I'm a good worker. I'm so good, they should make *me* the boss! Ha! But if you're trying to find the murderer, Ned, I'm not the one you should be talking to. You should talk to the woman who found the body."

"Who was that?" I asked.

"Natalie Rose," Kelly said. "She works the night shift. She starts around the same time everyone else leaves. In fact, if I hadn't been working late that night, I probably wouldn't have seen her."

"Why were you working late?" Alan asked. "I know we don't get paid overtime! Did you fall asleep during the day and have to catch up? Ha!"

"For your information, I was waiting on input from Mr. O'Neill," she said. "I had five different emails I needed him to respond to. I was going to forward his responses as soon as I got them, but he never got back to me, because...you know..."

That sounded a little suspicious to me. "If you needed something from Mr. O'Neill before you went home, why didn't you go into his office and ask him? I mean, his office is right next to your desk."

"I didn't want to disturb him," she said.

70

"You would rather stay late than upset him?"

"It wasn't a big deal. I had dinner scheduled for seven, so I could afford to work a little late."

"But staying a half-hour after you should be gone is pushing it," I argued.

"The only thing that's being pushed here is my patience. What I do after hours is *my* business, not yours. Do you have any more impertinent questions?"

Uh oh. She sounded angry. "Well...how did Natalie—?"

"That was a rhetorical question," Kelly snapped. "You've signed the paperwork, so there's nothing left for you to do here. I think you should take your baby and go."

I patted McKenzie. "Come on, McKenzie," I said loudly, "time for us to leave! You want to supervise me, Alan?"

"Oh, yeah! Sure!" he said. "Don't worry. I'll make sure he doesn't steal any office supplies! HA!"

Kelly looked suspicious, as Alan followed me out of the room. She was right to be suspicious. I still had more questions, and I picked Alan as an escort because he was talkative.

"How did Natalie discover the body?" I asked as Alan led me out.

"I don't know," he said. "I wasn't there, obviously, but I heard she was mad. *Real* mad."

"Oh, yeah?"

"Like, so mad, she marched down the row of cubicles and burst straight into the old man's office. Didn't even stop to get permission from Kelly first. And you know her, she guards his office door like a hawk."

She *did* stop me from entering the office without an appointment... "Why was Natalie so mad?"

"No idea. Like I said, I wasn't there. She entered the office, and three minutes later, she started screaming."

71

"She waited three minutes before she started screaming? Why?"

"She *claims* she didn't notice the body until then, but I think she's lying. No way would it take three minutes for someone to notice a corpse in a small office like that."

That certainly was true. It sounded like I would have to have a chat with Natalie Rose, but there was a minor problem: I had no idea who she was. I didn't work nights. Truth be told, I often slipped out of the office a few minutes early to ensure I would catch the bus on time.

"What happened next?" I asked.

"After Natalie screamed, Kelly rushed to the office. They called security and the police."

"And nobody else entered the office, right?"

"Not until the police came! And I heard that basically *everyone* in the building came to watch. I know *I* would want to know what's going on if one of my co-workers screamed."

"What about the time you dropped your keyboard on your hand?" Alan had screamed pretty loudly that day.

"That's different, and you know it," Alan said in a grumpy voice. "I told you a hundred times already, I was trying a new typing technique." That had been his official explanation when Mr. O'Neill asked, but I knew the truth. Alan had been goofing off and pretended the keyboard was a guitar, when he hurt himself.

We reached the exit at that point. "Thanks for all the info. One more question, though. How do you know all of this information? You said you weren't there when Natalie found the body."

"I have my sources. Secret sources. No, *special* sources! Secret, special sources that—"

"You were listening to gossip by the water cooler, weren't you?"

Alan looked ashamed again. "Well, yes, but that doesn't mean it's wrong!"

I groaned. In my experience, office gossip tended to be wrong more often than it was right. Or at least, the gossip was wrong about my baby's gender and name. When I came back to work after Brittany had given birth, I spent an entire week telling everyone that my baby was not named "Ned Junior".

I wondered what *really* happened when the body was discovered, because if no one killed O'Neill while everyone else was on break, Natalie was the prime suspect.

# Chapter 8

I checked my phone, before getting in the car. I had five new emails. One was from Brittany. She had shared a link to a website about three-month-old babies. I guess she thought I needed help with McKenzie. I didn't know whether to be grateful or insulted.

The other four emails were from my video service, saying more of my videos were flagged as inappropriate. That made six in one day. This was bad. Really, really bad. I already had *one* mystery on my hands. I didn't need another mystery to solve!

Figuring I should resolve the situation as soon as possible, I checked in with my tech guru. And by "my tech guru", I meant Scott. Like I said, he has a degree in computer engineering. I stopped by his work on the way home.

"Dude, you came in for pizza last night, and you're here again?" Scott asked. "I think you have a problem."

"I do have a problem, but it's not with your pizza," I said.

"Nobody has a problem with my pizza," he said proudly.

"It's a problem with my video channel. Someone keeps flagging my videos as inappropriate. I need to figure out who it is."

"Someone with a grudge against you? How am I supposed to know?"

"You're a computer wizard. Can you decode these number thingies on the emails?"

"Maybe. Let me see."

I handed over my phone, while he studied my emails.

His eyes narrowed, and he pushed his hat backwards on his head. "Huh, let me get my laptop for this." He went into his office and came back with a laptop. "Can I have your email and password?"

"Uh, *no*." He's my friend, but I wasn't about to trust him with my email password. I still remembered when he "borrowed" my phone, right before my wedding with Brittany. He posted ridiculous stuff on my social media accounts, and I didn't find out about it until after I came back from the honeymoon.

I logged onto my email server for him, and he went to work. He scanned the emails for a minute or two, muttering, "Huh. That's interesting."

"What's interesting?"

"All these videos were flagged at the same time. Yesterday, around six."

"That can't be right. I didn't get these emails yesterday. I got them today, all at different times."

"Yeah, but these are automated emails. They don't get sent right away." Scott played around on the computer some more, although I'm sure he wouldn't like hearing me call his work "playing". After a few minutes, he stopped. "I've got good news, and I've got bad news. Which one do you want to hear first?"

"Tell me the bad news."

"I can't tell who flagged your videos. The website's keeping their screen name private. Obviously, they don't want you to know."

"So some jerk can log on and flag all my videos, and there's nothing I can do about it?" I asked. "That's not fair!"

"It makes sense, though. If you knew who was doing it, you might harass them or try to get revenge or something. They don't want to encourage any vigilante justice."

That was *exactly* what I was planning on doing, but I felt like I probably shouldn't mention it. Instead, I asked, "What's the good news?"

"I managed to get their IP address. I did a reverse DNS on it to geolocate them."

"I don't know what that means."

Scott rolled his eyes at my lack of technical prowess. "Basically, I figured out where they were. They did it at the Lincoln Lake Library."

"The culprit is someone from *our* town?" That pretty much proved what I suspected: this wasn't a random coincidence. It was a personal attack, directed at me.

"Yeah, I guess," Scott said. "It'd be weird if someone came to our town, just to use the computer and mess with your videos."

"You're saying whoever flagged my videos was using the library computers?"

"Or their own computer, or a phone. All I know for sure is that they were using the library's wifi network at the time."

It sounded like the saboteur was trying to protect their identity by using a public network. "Well, thanks, Scott. You've given me a big clue. I guess my next step is to go to the library, and...wait."

"What's wrong?"

"My videos got flagged last night at the library? Are you *sure?*" I asked.

"Ninety percent sure. Why?"

"Don't you remember? Deirdre said she was meeting with the Mystery Club at the library at six! My videos are reviews for mystery books. They *have* to be responsible! The Mystery Club must be a cover for a group of foul criminals!"

Scott seemed unimpressed with my logic. "I think you're going a *bit* too far with this."

"I disagree. If anyone cares about my book reviews, it would have to be the Mystery Club. And Deirdre has disliked me ever since the two of us broke up."

"I don't think she'd try to sabotage your job, because of an old grudge."

"You're only saying that because you think she's hot," I snapped.

"And you don't?" Scott asked. He seemed legitimately confused that someone would question Deirdre's looks.

"I'm married. I'm not allowed to comment on how attractive my ex-girlfriends are," I explained. "Also, it's totally creepy for you to crush on my ex."

"I'm not crushing on her!" Scott said.

"I was here when you rang up her order last night. Did you, or did you not, give her a discount without telling her?"

"Dude! How did you know?"

I gestured towards the menu behind him. "The prices are listed right there. You didn't charge her for three extra-large pizzas."

"You're telling me you can do that math in your head, but you don't know what an IP address is?" Scott asked.

"Hey, I'm an accountant," I defended myself. "Or at least, I *was* an accountant until a few days ago." Scott was probably right, though. It wasn't like Deirdre to secretly sabotage me. I hated to admit it, but her videos were a lot more popular than mine. There was no need for her to sabotage me. I didn't pose any threat to her success. "Well, thanks again. McKenzie and I should get going."

"You're not gonna buy her a pizza?"

"Babies can't eat pizza." I readjusted McKenzie, and that's when I felt her diaper was larger than normal. Time for a diaper change! "Can I use the bathroom?"

"Bathrooms are for paying customers."

"It's not for me. It's the baby!"

"Oh. I guess that's okay, then."

"Thanks."

I went to the bathroom, but there wasn't a changing table in the men's room. I would have to change her on the sink counter. I took her there, but I could see there wasn't enough room to place her down. That meant I would either have to change her on the floor or on a toilet lid. Neither option appealed to me.

I poked my head out of the bathroom to complain, when I saw a changing tray sticker on the other bathroom door.

"Hey!" I shouted. "How come the women's room has a changing tray, but the men's room doesn't?"

"Because you're the only stay-at-home dad in town!" Scott called back at me.

"Oh, ha ha."

I went into the women's room, hoping that it would be empty, but it wasn't. I should've knocked first. There was a girl about four or five years old in there. Just my luck.

"What are *you* doing in here?" she asked. "This is for *girls!*"

I held McKenzie in front of me, like she was a protective shield. "She's a girl! I'm here to help her!"

"Aw, she's cute!" the girl said. "Can I help?"

"Do you know how to change diapers?"

"Ew! No!" She gave me a disgusted look, washed her hands, and left the bathroom. Phew. Potential disaster averted.

\* \* \*

Needless to say, I went to the Mystery Club meeting that night. It turned out that the Mystery Club was—let me be nice here—full of total weirdos. I should have known Deirdre wouldn't be part of a group of *normal* people.

They were meeting in the library's conference room. As soon as I stepped in, a man with a deerstalker cap and three coats pounced on me.

"Aha!" he said. "I see we have a visitor! A victim, perhaps? Or a culprit in disguise?"

"He has been robbed," said a large man with a fake mustache and an even faker accent. "He wants us to discover the culprit's identity."

"He's a murder victim," said a grim old woman in a colorful dress that greatly contrasted with her mood. "The kind with a secret. You think he was killed by accident, but no, he was part of a secret rebellion plotting to overthrow the local university."

"Excuse me?" I asked.

"I see by the way you're dressed that you're an American," said the Sherlock Holmes wannabe. He seemed inordinately proud of himself for making this deduction, as if meeting an American in America was something unusual. "Clearly, a banker who spends his nights visiting gambling-houses and..." He stopped cold, and his voice changed. "Doing drugs? That's going a bit too far!"

"What are you talking about?" I asked.

"The white powder on your shoulder. What sort of drug is it? A narcotic?"

"Marijuana, most likely," said the old woman.

"No, no, my friend," said the fake Frenchman. "You say this man is a rich banker. *I* say his fortune comes from the drugs which he smuggles, oh so neatly, into this country. Clearly, there is a woman involved."

I glanced at my shoulder. It had a white splotch on it, which must have been what got all of them riled up. "That's baby spit-up, not drugs."

"A poor excuse," said the Fake Frenchman.

"He's gonna get killed by a fellow drug-dealer," the old woman said. "Something bloody and violent, I hope! It's the only thing that can save this story."

"Am I missing something here?" I asked.

"Hello, everyone!" a cheerful voice said. Deirdre Simmons burst into the room, wearing a low-cut red dress which left little to the imagination. She embraced me in a deep hug. "And *hello*, my lovely—NED!" She noticed who she was touching, and jumped away from me, like it had caused her physical pain. "What the heck are *you* doing here?"

"I just wanted to see the Mystery Club!" I said. "Why did you hug me for no reason? And why are you dressed like *that?*"

Deirdre looked down at her dress and pulled it up as much as she could. "I'm the femme fatale, of course! If you checked the schedule, you would have known that tonight is cosplay night!"

"Cosplay night?"

"Where everyone is supposed to dress up like their favorite mystery character. We were going to make up our own mystery."

"I know what cosplay is, thanks," I said. So they all were play-acting? That made slightly more sense. I turned to the others. "Sorry, everyone! I didn't know I was supposed to pretend to be someone else."

"Huh, I thought you were Mark in disguise," Sherlock Holmes said.

"Mark is sick this week, remember?" the Fake Frenchman said.

"Unlikely! I bet he's been poisoned!" said the old woman. "Only no one will realize it, because he was stabbed before the poison took full effect! *Everyone* wanted to kill him!"

"Okay, I recognize the two male detectives," I muttered to Deirdre. "But who is the old woman dressed up as?"

"No one. She's like that normally," Deirdre said. She raised her voice so the others could hear. "You like murder mysteries, don't you, Kay?"

"Love 'em! The bloodier, the better!" she said, with way too much enthusiasm. It was nice to see senior citizens so...*passionate* about their hobbies.

"So you're a new member?" Sherlock Holmes said. "What's your name?"

"I'm Ned Gray," I said. "I, uh...I like mysteries."

"He's the guy I told you about yesterday," Deirdre said. "The one who reviews the Harvey Brothers books."

Fake Frenchman laughed. "Those aren't *real* mysteries."

"I'm going to pretend I did *not* just hear that *blasphemy*," I said. "The Harvey Brothers are the greatest detectives in the history of the world!"

"Please. They're a middle-class, white male fantasy from the 1950's," Deirdre said.

"They are from the *1920's*, and don't pretend that Francy Droo isn't *also* an outdated, gendered, stereotype-heavy fantasy," I said.

"Oh, those are fighting words," Deirdre said. "Francy Droo is better than the Harvey Brothers, any day."

"Francy Droo is a cheap knockoff of the Harvey Brothers, and you know it. Every single thing she achieved, the Harveys did first, ten years earlier."

"The only thing they achieved was chasing after loose women and fighting endless armies of mindless criminals."

"Loose women? That's rich, considering the way *you're* dressed right now. And some of those criminals were well-developed! They had...well, they had cool names!"

"Is *that* the only thing you like about the series? Bad guys with cool names?"

"No!" I said angrily. I was starting to remember why Deirdre and I broke up. We both found it too easy to fight with each other. "The Harveys use cool gadgets and *science* to solve crimes! Francy stumbles upon mystery solutions through pure luck!"

"The Harveys do *not* use science to solve crimes! They just beat up everyone they come across! That's violence, not science!"

"They do *too* use science! They built a science lab in their garage! How else are they supposed to figure out who the culprit is?"

"Oh, come on! The culprit's identity is always obvious! The culprit is always the one person who's mean to the Harveys! Every single time! You only need to read *one book* to know what the entire series is like!"

Kay started cackling. "I bet ten bucks she kills him, before he kills her!"

"A double murder, clearly," said the Fake Frenchman.

81

The interruption reminded me of where I was. "Sorry, I get a little defensive about the Harvey Brothers sometimes. My family doesn't think reviewing children's books counts as a *real* job."

"Ugh, my parents feel the same way," Deirdre said. "Like I'm not allowed to have hobbies? Please."

"Well, I don't think anyone else is coming tonight," Sherlock Holmes said. "Since you're our visitor, why don't you introduce yourself?"

"As I said before, I'm Ned Gray," I said. "I'm an accountant—I mean, I'm a stay-at-home dad, full time. I just started this week."

"You sure you can watch a kid by yourself?" Kay asked.

"Yes!" I said. "Why does everyone always ask that?"

"Oxytocin," Kay said.

"Excuse me?"

"It's a pleasure hormone that gets released whenever you hold an infant. It causes people to develop an emotional bond with their children. Oxytocin affects women way more than it affects men."

"Oh." I had never heard of oxytocin before. "How do you know this?"

"It was the main clue in *Death to Newborns*," Kay said. "You'd love that book. It's about a serial killer who murders all the babies in town."

I made a mental note to *never* read that mystery. At least, not until McKenzie was grown up.

The other Mystery Club members introduced themselves. Sherlock Holmes was actually a gas station attendant who read mysteries during slow hours. The Fake Frenchman was a construction worker who had caught the mystery bug while acting in a mystery play in junior high school. As for Kay Carlson, she was just an older woman who loved violent stories.

Deirdre introduced herself, even though there was no need. I knew she first got into mystery books because of me. I loaned her a *Francy Droo and Harvey Brothers Super Mystery* when we were first dating. You know, back in the phase when you pretend to like everything your partner likes. Come to think of it, she had never returned that book.

"I don't really read any mysteries, besides the Harvey Brothers," I admitted. "I'm pretty busy, but I *do* have a real-life mystery to solve. Two of them, actually. The first one is that someone has been flagging my videos as inappropriate."

"You've been uploading dirty videos?" Deirdre asked. "The scandal!"

"*No,*" I said angrily. "I mean the Harvey Brothers reviews. And I have good reason to believe the culprit is someone in this room."

They all looked at each other.

"Is this is a joke?" Sherlock Holmes asked. "Why would any of us care about your book reviews?"

"I only read adult mysteries," Kay said. "Like *Death in the White House.* Oh, that one was great! The President is having an affair with the Senate Minority Leader, so his wife smashes his brains in with a copy of the Constitution. Serves the cheater right! You can't have gory stories like that in kids books."

"Besides, the Dictionary Dan series is a much better mystery series for kids," Fake Frenchman said.

Deirdre looked upset. "I know I have to be your prime suspect, but I am *not* that petty. I was here in this room for the entire meeting yesterday. Everyone will support me on this."

"How did you know it happened during yesterday's meeting?" I asked.

"Because if it had happened earlier, you would have mentioned it when I saw you at the pizza place," Deirdre said. "And if it didn't happen during our meeting, you wouldn't have come here to investigate the Mystery Club members."

"You're right," I said. Wow. There was no fooling Deirdre. "How'd you figure that out by yourself?"

"You're not the *only* detective in this town," Deirdre said haughtily. "But you're barking up the wrong tree if you're accusing me or my friends."

"Yeah, we *solve* crimes, not commit them," Sherlock Holmes snapped.

"Okay, okay, I believe you!" I said. "For now. The second mystery is a lot more important, anyway." I described the murder of Mr. O'Neill to them. Being the mystery fans they were, they listened attentively and noted every small detail of the case without saying a word.

I'm joking, of course. It didn't take long for them to interrupt me with their theories as to what had happened.

"Kelly did it, without a doubt," Kay said. "She stayed late, because she needed someone to pin the crime on. Only a murderer would work unpaid overtime."

"Please," Sherlock Holmes said. "If she needed a fall guy, she would have used Ned."

"Sounds like she already tried to," Fake Frenchman said. "No, it's gotta be Natalie Rose. The mysterious third party that no one knows about. She only *pretended* to discover the crime scene to cast suspicion off of herself."

"For the sake of argument, I'll have to say it's Barry Wells," Sherlock Holmes said. "Notice how everyone's accusing *you* of being the last one to see the victim, when he was there at the same time you were. If no one is accusing him, it's because he covered his tracks well."

"Please, it's obviously this Alan loser," Deirdre said. "Who else would have a good motive to frame Ned? No offense, Ned, but it sounds like the two of you openly dislike each other."

"He's not violent enough to kill someone with a three-hole punch," Kay said. "You want someone with anger issues. It's Kelly. O'Neill broke one of the rules and she snapped."

"So...none of you agree on who the culprit is?" I asked.

They all shook their heads.

"Then how do I know who the killer is?"

"Investigation, obviously," Sherlock Holmes said. "Did you check the crime scene for clues? Since it was an unplanned murder, the culprit almost certainly left behind some evidence."

"Sorry, they didn't let me look at the crime scene," I said. "And since I don't work there anymore, I'll probably never get a chance to see it."

Sherlock looked discouraged. "Well...if you can't investigate on your own, I guess your best option right now is to talk to Detective Dodd and see if he has any new information."

"Yeah, that would be the next logical step," Fake Frenchman said. "Contact the detective in charge of the investigation."

"I don't have his contact info," I said. "I could call the station and ask for it, I guess, but I don't want to be rude."

Everyone in the room groaned.

"Ned, we read mysteries all the time for fun," Deirdre said. "You get a chance to solve a *real-life mystery*, and you're not jumping on it? You'll never join the Mystery Club with that attitude."

I wasn't sure I *wanted* to join the Mystery Club, to be honest. "Sorry?"

"It's okay," Deirdre said. "You can make it up to us by being the murder victim."

"Excuse me?"

"It's *cosplay night*, and I didn't dress up like this for nothing!" Sherlock Holmes said. "Now, how will we kill him?"

"Gunshot to the head," Fake Frenchman said.

"Too quick," Kay said. "How about drowning?"

"I have some *great* ideas," Deirdre said, smiling. "We can begin by stabbing him in the chest, then—"

"I have to go to the bathroom!" I said loudly. Then I ran away from the Mystery Club as quickly as my legs would take me. I hadn't solved the mystery of who demonetized my videos, but at least I had escaped alive.

# Chapter 9

Before leaving the library, I checked to see if they had any good cookbooks. Something fancy that would impress my wife and show her that I am totally on top of this stay-at-home dad thing. I opened up the fanciest looking book of the bunch and saw that it had a bunch of recipes I couldn't pronounce.

I put it back and went with one of the quick and easy cookbooks instead. It had a recipe for roast chicken. I was interested, until I saw that it had twelve different steps. Clearly, the author and I have different ideas about the definition of "quick and easy". *My* idea of an easy recipe looked something like this:

*Step 1: Buy food in a box.*
*Step 2: Follow the instructions on the box.*
*Step 3: Enjoy!*

I ended up getting a few cookbooks, in hopes that one of them would work. I had, uh...okay, this is embarrassing to admit, but I had totally screwed up on dinner that night. I wasn't sure which foods went with each other, and I couldn't find our grocery list in order to make sure.

I had tried to make spicy beef burritos. We had tortillas and beef, as well as some spicy orange sauce which looked kind of like queso. I figured it made sense, but when my wife came home from work, she disagreed.

Brittany told me the orange sauce was for chicken tikka masala. Even a bad cook like me knows that you don't put *chicken* sauce on *beef.* The food ended up being fine, even if it tasted a little off, but Brittany had made so many jokes about it, I was determined not to have any more cooking disasters.

She was waiting for me, when I got home. "You're back early," she said. "I thought the meeting was supposed to go until seven."

"I, um...left early," I said.

"Why?"

"Let's just say the people there weren't very helpful," I sighed.

"Too bad you're a stay-at-home dad, not a stay-at-home detective. You want to talk about it?"

I looked at her and smiled. "You know I do."

"Great!" Brittany smiled back at me, and I felt the urge to kiss her for being so wonderful to me. "Earlier, you told me you went into the office today. What did you find out?"

"Not much. Apparently *everyone* went on break at the exact same time that day."

"And let me guess. That's when the murder took place," she said.

"I actually don't know when the murder was," I said. "The police haven't made the autopsy results public yet."

"And if they do, you're not going to be the first person they call."

"That's sad, but true. Still, I'm betting the murder took place then. It's the only time someone could have gotten past Kelly without being seen."

"Unless *she* did it. Does she have a motive?"

"Pretty much everyone has a motive," I said bluntly. "Mr. O'Neill was a jerk."

"Yeah, but he's been a jerk to everyone for months. If that's the only reason for murder, why kill him *now?* Why didn't the murderer kill him much earlier?"

"You're right. Maybe they were waiting for a good opportunity to pin the crime on someone else." Namely me. "Or maybe there's a motive we don't know about. Like, O'Neill discovered Kelly and Barry have a secret relationship. Or he caught Alan embezzling funds. He hinted that the company was having financial problems."

"What kind of financial problems?" Brittany asked.

"I don't know exactly, but everything indicates that Mr. O'Neill was planning to fire someone, to save the company money. That sounds like a last-ditch effort to boost our revenue."

"Can I just say it's weird that your accounting firm has finance problems? Like, if you were all good at your jobs, this would never happen."

"Tell me about it," I said. I wondered who Mr. O'Neill was planning to fire. Not me, obviously. If he had been planning to fire me, he would have mentioned it when he *did* fire me. Maybe Barry? His job was the least essential to the company's business, after all.

"The other possibility is that he was killed much later, when Natalie found the body," I said.

"I don't know who that is."

"I looked her up on social media." Luckily, Alan was friends with *every* employee at our company, so finding her online was easy. "I *think* I met her once, at a company event. She works the night shift. Like, on purpose. She's a college student, so she can't work during the day."

"One person on your team works the night shift?" Brittany asked. "That's some weird scheduling. You would think it'd be hard for her to do her job without any co-workers to help with anything. Plus, she'd always be forced to wait a day, before anyone answered her emails."

"Yeah, but on the plus side, she gets to avoid dealing with Alan all the time," I said. "He was the one who told me about her. I'm pretty sure I can't trust him on this, but he says she went into the office and waited three minutes, before screaming for help."

"How'd she get in the office, if it was locked?"

"I...I don't know," I said. "That's a really good point. I bet Alan got it wrong."

"An unreliable witness, huh?" Brittany glanced at McKenzie to make sure she was doing fine—she was—then she looked back at me. "I know Alan is annoying, but he likes you. Why would he lie to you about what happened?"

"It's not so much lying, as it is Alan being Alan. He gets things wrong a lot. Remember last month, when Alan told everyone that the company was going to be bought by an art gallery? Or the time he thought his wife was O'Neill in disguise?"

"You didn't tell me about that."

"Oh my gosh, it was the stupidest thing ever. O'Neill said something that set Alan off during one of our weekly staff meetings. I'm in the cubicle next to him, so I had to hear him complain about it *every single day*. 'That's what my wife says! Nobody uses that phrase besides her! That couldn't have been O'Neill! Do you think it was my wife in disguise?' I had to tell him a million times that I didn't know, and I didn't care."

"That sounds weird. Is there any *reason* his wife would try to dress up like your boss?"

"I don't know," I said. I gave up trying to follow Alan's logic a long time ago. "Nothing got resolved until the next staff meeting. Alan was squirming in his seat the whole time, until the end, when O'Neill asked if there were any questions. Alan asked point blank if O'Neill was wearing a disguise. O'Neill kicked him out of the meeting."

"I hadn't thought about it, but that's a huge downside to getting promoted," Brittany said. "What if I get an employee like him? Or someone unmanageable who brings down the whole group? I got this job because I'm good with numbers, not because I'm good with people."

"Hey, I'm proud of you and your promotion," I said. "As long as none of your employees try to kill you, you should be fine."

"Thanks for the vote of confidence, but I'm still worried. What if I don't—?"

She was interrupted when McKenzie pooped and started whimpering. I could smell the poop almost immediately. Yuck.

"I'll get that," Brittany said. She truly is the best wife ever.

She changed McKenzie's diaper and brought it back with her. "I'm going to throw this out," she said, holding it up. "Are the diapers on the counter clean?"

"Huh? Oh, no, they're dirty. Those are from earlier today."

Brittany sighed and pinched her forehead. "Why did you make a pile of dirty diapers on the kitchen counter instead of throwing them away?"

"I'm sorry, I forgot. I'll clean them up right away." I gathered all the diapers in my arms and carried them outside to the trashcan. As usual, the trashcan was starting to look a little full. Maybe we needed to get a second trashcan, one that's just for diapers. And when McKenzie is potty trained, we can burn it.

By the time I came back inside, Brittany was sitting on the floor, playing with the baby. "So what else happened today?" she asked.

"I met your best friend Jessica."

"Ugh. She was at baby playtime?"

"Barely. She dropped her kid off and ran away. The other moms made it seem like she does that all the time."

"She does. She basically treats us like free baby-sitting. Good thing her kid is nice."

That wasn't at all how I would describe him. "Are we talking about the same kid? The scary one who looks like he's a bouncer-in-training?"

"No, I mean the cute blonde boy. He needs a haircut, though."

"Yeah, that's the one," I said. "He wouldn't leave me alone during the playtime, even when I moved him somewhere else."

"Aw, the little boy wouldn't leave you alone? That's cute."

"Not really! He kept growling at me, and he even hit me! It's like he wanted to fight me or something."

"Well, he's probably just intimidated by you," Brittany said. "You're probably the first male he's met that isn't a total loser. The only men he knows are Jessica's boyfriends, and Lord knows his father isn't anywhere in the picture."

Just like last night, Brittany's words sounded unnecessarily vindictive. "Is there a reason why you hate Jessica so much?" I asked. "I agree she's kind of sleazy, but you're acting like it's personal."

"She reminds me of Elizabeth," Brittany said. Seeing the blank look on my face, she added, "Sorry, you don't know who that is. That's the girl my boyfriend cheated on me with, before I started dating you. I know that was years ago at this point, but...I guess it still makes me a little angry."

Brittany had told me before that her ex cheated on her, but she hadn't given me any details. I figured it wasn't any of my business. "I understand," I said. "I still feel a little awkward around Deirdre, even though we broke up in high school."

Brittany didn't want to talk any more after that, so I let her play with the baby while I went into our room and read *Harvey Brothers #127: The Kidnapped Baby-Sitters*. The book was totally not the way I remembered it. I thought it was a book all about kids and infants, but it turned out they were barely in the story. In fact, the baby-sitter angle was mostly an excuse for the Harveys to meet hot chicks.

Let me quote the book here, to show what I'm talking about. This is the part where I stopped reading:

*"You baby-sit a lot?" Fred asked the beautiful collegiate.*

*"All the time!" she said. Bess tucked her hair behind her ear, and Fred couldn't help but notice how wonderful her skin looked in the afternoon sun.*

*"Aren't you afraid of being attacked by the kidnapper, though?" Jim interrupted. Fred shot him an annoyed glance. You shouldn't interrupt your brother when he's flirting.*

*"Hmmm...maybe I am," Bess said. She shot a brilliant smile at Fred. "Why don't you come with me on my next sitting job? You can protect me if any bad guys show up!"*

*"Me, baby-sit? No way! I'm a guy! I can't watch kids!" Fred protested.*

*"No, but you can watch me," Bess said. "The kids go to bed at eight, and I need something to do until the parents get back at ten. What do you say?"*

*"I would love be with you," Fred said. "I mean, I'd love to."*

Bess giggled, and I groaned. I knew these books were old-fashioned, but I didn't expect them to say outright that men can't handle watching children. Talk about anti-stay-at-home dad prejudice! I made a note to complain about that in my review of the book.

91

There was *one* good idea in the book, though. It described a bouncy horse game, where you put the baby on your legs and bounce her up and down by bending your knees. I decided to try it out, myself. I took McKenzie into her room and bounced her. I was a little worried it would hurt McKenzie's neck, but she seemed to love it. She let out a loud gasp, then laughed once.

I stopped cold. "Did you just laugh?"

She smiled at me, and I bounced her up again. She laughed again. Her first laugh!

"Oh, McKenzie!" I said. I gave her a hug. I got to hear her first laugh! "Brittany, did you hear that?"

"Hear what?" Brittany called from the other room.

"She laughed! Listen!"

I tried bouncing her again, but all she did was breathe heavily. Apparently, those two laughs were all she had, but that was okay. I was satisfied.

"I love you," I whispered to McKenzie. And that was when I first truly believed that I made the right choice in becoming a stay-at-home dad.

Brittany appeared at the doorway. "She laughed? Are you sure?"

"Yes. I was bouncing her up and down and she *laughed!*"

Brittany brushed her behind her shoulder. "That's amazing. Babies aren't supposed to laugh until they're four months old. She must really love you."

"I love her, too," I said. Forget Jessica, Deirdre and the murder investigation. This had been my best day ever.

* * *

My great day continued, as McKenzie slept through the entire night. *In her crib.* That's right; she didn't have to be moved into our bed, like she normally did. First laughing, then sleeping through the night? It was like she grew up one month, in one day!

I woke up at 6:30 a.m., feeling extra-refreshed. I promptly got out of bed and made myself a breakfast of cereal, eggs, and toast.

I'm kidding, of course. I woke up and went right back to sleep, until the baby started crying for her morning diaper change. Morning diapers are the worst; they swell up to the size of basketballs.

No, scratch that. The *worst* is when you wake up in the middle of the night, only to find that the last diaper wasn't put on correctly. Because, hey, it turns out that it's not easy to put a diaper on a squirming infant in a dark room at 4:00 a.m.. Who knew?

Still, the extra-large diaper gave me an idea. What if they made double-layer diapers? Like, a diaper that goes on over the other diaper. That way, you only have to swap one diaper out at a time. You'd get away with only changing diapers *half* as often!

I shook my head. These are the weird ideas you get when you need more sleep. Also, when you spend the entire day by yourself, with nobody else to talk to. I like McKenzie more than ever now, but she's not a good conversationalist. That's probably why I found myself fantasizing about talking to Brittany every night.

Yes, *that* is what I fantasize about doing with my wife. Being a stay-at-home dad does weird things to you.

Other weird things? I spent way too much time thinking about nipples. We have over six bottles for McKenzie, and they all have different-shaped nipples. I keep trying to figure out which one works best. At one point, I decided to time it, to see which one takes the least amount of time for her to drink from, but my plans got derailed when McKenzie threw a screaming fit. I wonder if professional science experiments ever get cancelled due to screaming infants.

Also, I began to obsess over the term "stay-at-home dad". Stay-at-home dad. Stay at home dad. Does it sound better with or without the hyphens in between the words? Should the "dad" be capitalized? For a while, I thought about calling myself a "stay-at-home parent", but I realized the acronym for that was "STAHP". Like, someone shouting "stop" in an angry voice. I guess I'd rather be SAHD than STAHP.

Anyway, I'm totally rambling now. Sorry about that. The point is that I spent most of Thursday morning thinking about my life and how it had changed so drastically that week. I probably would have kept going in that vein for another half-hour, except I noticed a piece of paper sticking out from under the front door.

*Weird. Nobody's ever slid a note under our door before,* I thought. Curious as to what was going on, I picked it up and read it. Here's what it said:

*Ned,*

*Leave O'Neill's death alone, or you'll wind up DEAD, just like him!*

# Chapter 10

A threatening message! I'll admit that I screamed when I read it, but in my defense, it was a deep, manly scream. At least, compared to McKenzie's.

I had no idea this sort of thing happened in real life! I thought it only happened in *Harvey Brothers* books! I had read enough to know that, as a general rule, each book has two threatening messages, a threatening phone call, five near-death experiences, and two fakeout culprit attacks. (Sometimes, the original series was formulaic, that way.)

The culprit had left me a threat! It had to be the culprit, right? No one else would want to scare me off the case.

Was I scared? No. Well, kind of. No! No, I was *not* scared! This was just a cheap trick, designed to fool the faint of heart! I wasn't going to fall for it!

I wasn't going to drop the investigation, not when I was so close to finding the culprit! Because I *was* close to finding the culprit...right? True, I had absolutely no idea who the culprit was, but if the culprit went to such great lengths to scare me, that must have meant that I was getting close to solving the case.

I meant "great lengths" literally. Whoever left this message had to have travelled at least a half-hour to do so. None of my co-workers live near me. At least, I don't *think* they do. I'd have to check social media to be sure, but my commute to work was an hour-long bus ride. It's a safe bet to say I wasn't in the same neighborhood as the others.

I tried examining the piece of paper for clues, but I didn't find any. As far as I could tell, someone printed out the message on a computer, using a standard piece of paper. There wasn't a whole lot to go on.

I began to wonder if any of my co-workers knew my address. Had any of them visited my house before? I got excited for a moment when I realized only Kelly had access to my personnel files—if she was the only one who could have done it, she *must* be the culprit—but then I remembered that everyone had access to the company directory. It was built in to the email system. The idea was to make it so that you could find anyone's work email in case you forgot what it was, but hypothetically, it could be used to send someone a threat like this.

Too bad I didn't have access to the email system anymore. Then I'd be able to see who looked up my address in the directory, recently. I had no idea *how* to do that, but I'm sure Scott did. I could ask him to check for me. That's one of the benefits of having your own personal tech guru/pizza chef.

I reread the note. I noticed it said "O'Neill", instead of "Mr. O'Neill". Was that a clue? Was the culprit on familiar terms with Mr. O'Neill? Granted, everyone knew who he was, but some people (like me) usually called him *Mister* O'Neill. It seemed to make him happy to be called that. I always figured it was an empowerment thing.

I thought about the threatening message for the rest of the morning. Was the threat serious or not? Was the culprit actually plotting to kill me, or was it just an empty threat, designed to scare me? How could you tell the difference?

It was so stressful, it almost made me wish I could go back a half-hour, when the only thing I worried about was being a stay-at-home dad. *Almost.* Which reminded me, I still hadn't told my parents about my career change. I checked my phone and decided nah, there wasn't enough time to call them. Baby playtime would start in an hour; I needed to get ready right away.

I'm only half-joking. If the baby decided she would need a bottle, that could easily eat up a half-hour, especially if I had to change her clothes or diaper afterwards. I know *some* people claim they can change a baby's diaper in under a minute. You know what I call those people? Liars.

I decided to make some formula, just in case McKenzie was hungry. While I was in the middle of doing that, it suddenly hit me: my ex-girlfriend, Deirdre. *She* must have left the threatening message. She must have thought it was a hilarious prank.

Did she know where I lived? If she didn't, she could have learned by following me home from the library. That would have been creepy, but it was the only logical explanation. No one else involved in the case had the opportunity to do this. Not unless they were *really* desperate and scared that I would solve the mystery, and if I'm being honest, that's unlikely. I don't think I'm *that* much of a threat. Especially since I'm more or less unable to go back to work.

It turned out McKenzie didn't want any formula, so I put the bottle into my diaper bag. I figured we could play tummy time. That's the game where you lie the baby down on her stomach, then leave her like that for a while. Brittany has a special song for it:

*It's tummy time!*
*It's tummy time!*
*It's tummy tummy tummy time!*
*Oh yes! Oh yeah! Tummy tummy tummy time!*

Yeah, it's another song for babies which is basically the same three words, over and over again. I tried to distract myself from the threatening note, by coming up with a different tummy time song:

*Don't be a dummy,*
*It's time for the tummy!*
*You're in the zone*
*When you're lying prone!*
*You don't rest supine*
*'Cause it's tum-my time!*
*Uh...You don't mess around*
*When you're lying down?*

That was about as far as I got. It's official: I am terrible at coming up with songs. My apologies to anyone who was looking forward to me releasing a baby song album.

Tummy time was not very interesting that morning. McKenzie didn't seem to notice that she was on her stomach. She just lay on the ground with her eyes closed, like she was sleeping. Her head was turned to the left, so she could breathe freely.

After a minute or two, I said, "Hey, McKenzie. You're supposed to be having tummy time right now. What's wrong?"

97

McKenzie's eyes opened. She flapped her left arm towards me and tried to lift her neck. That's the main reason you're supposed to do tummy time: it helps develop arm and neck muscles, in preparation for crawling. McKenzie started crying.

"Try again. You can lift your head up higher than that!"

McKenzie started screaming.

"Okay, tummy time is over!" I picked her up and calmed her down with a different game—"Let's put on silly hats!"—until it was time to leave for baby playtime. Going to this group was starting to become the highlight of my day. In college, if you had told me my life would come to this in less than ten years, I never would have believed you.

Movie Star Mom was there, and she was wearing a full-length red dress that matched her hair. It looked great on her, but I don't think it's practical to wear a dress when you spend most of your day crawling after an infant. She was chatting with Crazy Hair, who had the left half of her head in a side ponytail. It stuck out so far, I wondered if she ever hit someone with her hair accidentally.

The Jennifers were there, along with a new mom. All three of them were wearing matching mom jeans and sleeve tops, so I could only assume she was also part of the Jennifer Club. I sat down next to them and listened as the three of them talked about baby names.

"Luminous or L'Arachel for a girl, obviously," Jennifer #1 said. "Maybe L'Engle or Leopold for a boy."

"You can't be serious," Jennifer #2 said. "The kid wouldn't be able to spell those until she's in fifth grade!"

"Yeah, I would go with something more common, like Luke," Jennifer #1 said. "You know, like the *Star Wars* character."

"Oh, I *love* those movies!" Jennifer #3 said. "For about a month, we thought we were going to name our daughter Leia."

"I totally get it," I said. "If we had a boy instead of a girl, I would have named him Jar-Jar Chewbacca Kenobi."

98

The Jennifers glared at me, while Workout Mom let out a snicker. At least *someone* liked my stupid dad jokes. I readjusted McKenzie's clothes, and I heard two loud voices arguing the hallway.

"I'm telling you, you can't do that!"

"I don't *care* what you think, you fat loser! You're just jealous because I don't smell like diapers all day long!"

"Because you never watch your own kid!"

A furious Jessica entered the room, arguing with Sleeping Woman. I was surprised to see her awake, and even more surprised to see her chewing Jessica out. "Raising a child is hard work, but you've never bothered to do any work, a single day of your life!"

"Work is for poor people," Jessica said.

"And I suppose you *worked* for your family fortune?" Sleeping Woman asked.

"Uh, duh! I had to suck up to my parents *all the time* when I was growing up!" Jessica said. "Do you know how hard it is to care about boring adult stuff? Moving out of state was the best decision I ever made."

"You *are* an adult! Start acting like one!"

"I will, when you *stop* acting like my mom!" Jessica said. She put her toddler on the ground. "I'm going to get a *coffee!*" she announced to no one in particular, then she left the room.

Sleeping Woman let out an angry growl. "I *hate* that woman!"

The other moms made sympathetic noises, and McKenzie started crying. She was probably startled by the shouting match. I tried soothing her, when I noticed her diaper was wet.

I got up to change her. The bathrooms are on the far end of the hall. I didn't see Jessica anywhere, which I suppose was for the best. Truth be told, I was kind of hoping to run into her and learn what had started her fight with Sleeping Woman.

Once again, the men's room didn't have a changing tray for babies. I peeked into the women's bathroom, and sure enough, there was a changing tray there. *When are they going to have gender equality for bathroom changing trays?* I wondered.

I changed McKenzie's diaper, when I discovered a new problem. The hand-washing sink and towel dispenser were on the far side of the room. I didn't want to leave McKenzie alone while I went across the room to wash my hands, but I didn't want to put on her clothes with dirty hands, either.

Clearly, there was only one solution: play basketball.

I rolled up McKenzie's diaper into a ball and tossed it from hand to hand. "Ned takes the ball and dodges left. Oh, he's being screened! He dodges right, not enough room! Time is running out! Can he do it? He pulls back to make a three-pointer..."

I took a step back and aimed for the trash can on the other side of the room. I threw the diaper-ball across the room, and of course, that's when someone opened the door.

It was Jessica. She noticed me right away. "What are you—?" she began to say, when the diaper hit her face.

"Oops! Sorry! My aim was a little off."

"You freak! You *pervert!*" she shouted. "You shouldn't be in the women's room, anyway! How dare you throw this—this—this *disgusting thing* at me!"

"It's just a folded up diaper. I'm sure you change your son's diapers all the time."

"Are you *crazy?!* Who *does* that?! I want you out of here, *right now!*"

"I still have to wash my hands."

Jessica screamed and left the room.

"Please don't be like her when you grow up, kiddo," I told McKenzie. "I don't think I could handle it." I finished cleaning up McKenzie and washed my hands. This time, I dropped the paper towels into the trash can instead of throwing them. My wannabe basketball shots had caused more than enough trouble for one day.

When I got back to the baby playtime group, I found Jessica yelling about me.

"—sick weirdo!" she said. "You *have* to kick him out immediately!"

"I told you, this group is free to everyone," Workout Mom said calmly. She motioned towards me. "Here he is now. Ned, Jessica has been making complaints about you—"

"You threw a dirty diaper at my head!" Jessica said.

"Can you explain what happened?" Workout Mom asked.

I started to worry that I was in big trouble. What if they kicked me out of baby playtime? Not only would it be super embarrassing to be ejected from an infant group, but I wouldn't have anything to do every day at eleven o'clock.

"It was an accident!" I said. "I was trying to throw the diaper in the trash can. Jessica just got in the way."

"Why would you throw a diaper all the way across the room?" Workout Mom asked.

I wasn't sure how to respond. It would sound stupid if I said I was pretending to play basketball. Luckily, one of the Jennifers came to my defense. "The trash can *is* on the other side of the room from the changing tray. It's hard to reach."

"So move the trash can somewhere else!" Jessica said. "You shouldn't have been in the women's restroom in the first place! It's the *women's* room! Not *women and creepy diaper-loving weirdos* room!"

"There isn't a changing tray in the men's room, though," I said. "I can't change my baby's diaper on the floor. That's unsanitary!"

"No, what's *unsanitary* is throwing baby poop at someone's face!" Jessica said.

"The diaper was rolled up. Only the outside of it touched your face," I said. "And besides, it was a pee diaper."

"I'm still *filthy and disgusting!* It's going to take me *all day* to clean this mess off of me! So what are you going to do about it?" She put her hands on her hips and glared at me. She probably expected me to pay for a free spa day or something.

I decided to lighten the mood with a dad joke. Reaching into my diaper bag, I pulled out some baby wipes. "Here! You can use these to clean off!"

The Jennifers started laughing, and Jessica screamed. "I demand you kick him out, *now!*"

"Look, this seems like an accident," Workout Mom said. "Let's set a good example for the children and apologize like—"

"I am never coming back here again!" Jessica screamed. She called me a naughty word that you shouldn't use around children, then she picked up her toddler and marched out of the room.

"Did you just get rid of her *for good?*" Jennifer #1 asked.

Sleeping Woman started clapping. "You are my new hero."

"No more Jessica!" Jennifer #2 cheered.

Workout Mom shook her head. "You shouldn't cheer because someone else is upset, even if it's Jessica. We have to set a good example for the babies, you know. Still...thanks, Ned. Jessica's been a minor problem for our group for a while."

"Yeah, thanks," Movie Star Mom said. "I knew having a guy in the group would be good for us."

I smiled. Who knew angering Jessica by accident would make me popular? I should pretend to be good at sports more often.

The moms continued to be nice to me for the rest of the day. It was so good, I decided to stay afterwards, instead of leaving right away. It felt like I was now an official member of the baby playtime group, instead of the awkward guy who hid in the corner all the time. My wife would be proud.

A little before noon, my phone rang. I half-expected it to be Brittany, but when I checked it, Detective Dodd's name was staring at me.

"We don't encourage cell phone use at baby playtime," Workout Mom said. "The goal is to focus on the children, not our devices."

"I have to take this," I said.

"No, you don't," Workout Mom said.

"But it's the police!"

"Yeah, right," Jennifer #3 said.

"That's the lamest excuse I've ever heard," Jennifer #1 said.

"I'm one hundred percent serious!" I said. "Look, I—hey!"

Workout Mom took the phone from my hands and hit the "answer" button. She made a point of putting it on speaker, so everyone else could hear the conversation. That was more than a little embarrassing.

"I'm sorry, I can't talk right now," she said.

"Mr. Gray. You're sounding different today," Detective Dodd said.

"I'm answering for him," Workout Mom said. "He's busy."

"I didn't know stay-at-home dads had people who screened their calls. Unless the baby has suddenly learned how to talk?"

"This is Sara Benson. I'm in charge of baby playtime here at the Lincoln Lake Community Center."

"And this is Detective Rene Dodd of the Portland Police. I'd appreciate it if you let me talk to my murder suspect, thank you."

Workout Mom dropped the phone in surprise. "Jessica called the police on you!"

"I *told* you it was the police!" I said.

"No way! You can't get arrested for throwing a diaper at someone's head!" Jennifer #1 said. "At least, I don't *think* so..."

"Jessica must have embellished the story," Sleeping Woman said.

Workout Mom's baby crawled to my phone. Workout Mom picked up both. "You should *take the call*, before the police come to *arrest you!*" she said in her sing-songy baby voice. "That would be *bad!* It'd interrupt *block-building time!*"

I grabbed the phone and stood up. I made sure to turn it *off* of speaker mode. "Hello, Detective Dodd. Sorry for the confusion. I'm at baby playtime right now, and they don't encourage cell phone use."

"So I gathered," Dodd said. "What's this I hear about you trying to kill someone with a diaper?"

"I didn't try to kill her with a diaper! I just...threw a diaper at a trash can, and her head got in the way."

"Excitement seems to follow you around, Mr. Gray," Dodd said, "but I've got something to talk about which is a bit more important than dirty diapers."

"The murder?"

"Yes. I want you to come back to the office today at two o'clock. If you've got other plans, cancel them. You don't want to miss this."

"You figured out who the murderer is?"

"Not yet, but there's new evidence I need to discuss with everyone. Let's just say there's a photograph of John Jerkley hiding the money in a secret compartment."

It took a few seconds for me to register his reference. "You read the first *Harvey Brothers* book?"

"I've read all of them. I loved those books as a kid. I saw your review of it yesterday—"

"You get *paid* to watch online videos?" I exclaimed.

104

"I was *investigating the suspects!*" Dodd snapped. "Your file says you work with mysteries in your side job. It could have been relevant to the case."

"I have a police file?" I asked. That was an unpleasant surprise.

Dodd sighed. "I'm trying to do you a favor here, Mr. Gray. Please don't make me regret this."

"I'm sorry," I said, although I wasn't sure what I was apologizing for.

"Good. I got the results from the lab back. Since you're a fan of mystery books, so I figured you'd like to be here when I went over the evidence with everyone."

"I would love that!"

"Good. Be here at two o'clock," he said. "Now if you'll excuse me, I need to check with my friends in the assault and battery department, to see if they've ever heard of 'attack by diaper'."

That was when I decided Detective Dodd wasn't such a bad person, after all. I hung up the phone, only to find myself confronted by a group of worried moms.

"Are you going to jail?" Jennifer #1 asked.

"Did I hear you mention *murder?*" Movie Star Mom asked.

"Why would a police officer be watching online videos?" Workout Mom asked.

"It's a long story," I said.

# Chapter 11

I couldn't wait to tell Brittany the news, so I called her in the parking lot. "You won't believe what just happened," I said excitedly.

Brittany laughed. "You got a threatening note from the culprit?"

Shoot. I had forgotten to mention that when Dodd called. That was important information! "I...How did you know?" I asked.

"I wrote it."

I almost dropped my phone when I heard this. "*You* left that threatening note?"

"Well, of course," Brittany said. "I thought you'd get a kick out of it. It's just like one of your books."

"So it was just a joke?" I asked. Some joke! It nearly gave me a heart attack. "How could you do something like that to me? I thought I was about to be murdered!"

"Really?"

"Well, maybe not," I admitted. "I figured Deirdre wrote it. But it *did* scare me."

"I guess that makes it a successful prank, then," Brittany said. "Sorry, Ned. I wasn't trying to scare you. I thought you'd see through it right away."

I paused for a moment. Maybe there was a lesson in this. Like, maybe you shouldn't rule out anyone as a suspect. Or maybe you shouldn't overthink things; the solution to the mystery could be a lot simpler than you'd expect. Or maybe the lesson was "I'm a bad detective, and I shouldn't try to solve mysteries".

...Hopefully that wasn't the real moral of the story.

"So if you're not calling about the note, what are you calling about?" Brittany asked.

"Detective Dodd called. I think I'm no longer a main suspect in Mr. O'Neill's murder."

"That's great news! Have they caught the real culprit?"

"Not yet," I said, "but there's a meeting at the office at 2:00, to talk about it."

"And naturally you're going, even though you're not an employee anymore."

"Of course."

"Well, you'll have to tell me all about it when you get home," Brittany said. "Also, you can tell me about, uh...where did you go last night?"

"The Mystery Club. Now that *didn't* go so well. But baby playtime did!"

"Oh yeah? Glad to hear you're finally starting to enjoy being with the other moms. What made it so good today?"

"I threw a dirty diaper at Jessica's head, and she quit baby playtime forever."

"No, really."

"I'm serious. I didn't throw the diaper at her on purpose, of course, but she was so angry, there was no reasoning with her."

"So, she quit?" Brittany asked.

"She threw an epic tantrum, and *then* she quit. The other moms were really happy with me, and they started treating me better. I feel like I'm finally starting to fit in."

"I'll *bet* they were happy. That's really great, Ned. I knew you could handle the stay-at-home dad thing. I just hope I can handle being a manager."

"I could throw diapers at your unruly employees," I offered generously.

"That's nice, Ned, but I think I'll stick to writing them anonymous threats, instead."

I laughed.

"I should get back to work," Brittany said. "Good luck with the rest of the day!"

"Love you!"

"Yes, I know I'm not supposed to take personal calls at work. I turned it off, okay?"

"Brittany?"

"I'm a good manager. But I'm not going to hang up whenever my husband calls. What if there's an emergency with the baby?"

"I CAN STILL HEAR YOU!" I shouted.

"Crap. Sorry, Ned! I hit the wrong button. Bye!"

This time, the call ended for real. It sounded like she was getting grief for accepting my call. That was harsh. No wonder she was worried about her promotion.

I drove back home, where I fed McKenzie and took a nap with her. I had lunch, and there was a little bit of playtime before we left for the meeting at my work. I made sure to arrive early, because I didn't want to miss a moment of what was going to happen.

A short blonde woman with giant glasses was sitting in the waiting area. Since Detective Dodd wasn't there yet, I took the waiting chair across from her.

"Your baby is cute," she said. "How old is she?"

"Three months," I said. "Her name is McKenzie."

"Hi, McKenzie! It's nice to meet you. My name is Natalie."

Uh oh. This wasn't a random nice woman! This was one of my suspects!

* * *

*Suspect Dossier*

Name: Natalie Rose

Occupation: Student by day, accountant by night.

Physical Description: Blonde, shorter than me. Wears giant glasses that make her eyes look larger than they are. They must help her work with computers when it's dark. Either that, or her fashion sense is even worse than mine.

Age: Early twenties? It'd be rude of me to ask.

Biggest Secret: Hasn't watched a movie in the past ten years.

Hobbies: Cell phone games, watching ice hockey.

Marital Status: Probably single. You can't have much of a dating life if you work all night and go to school all day.

Motive for Murder: Needs money to pay off her student loans.

* * *

"You're the one who found the body," I said.

"Uh...yes," she said. "And you are?"

"I'm Ned Gray," I said.

"The one who makes those online videos?"

"You know me?" I asked excitedly. My first real-life fan sighting!

"No, but Kelly told me about you. You were the last person to see Mr. O'Neill alive. Did the police call you here, so they can talk to you, too?"

"Yep, but I was hoping I could talk to you first."

"Why?" Natalie asked suspiciously.

"I'm trying to solve the mystery."

"You mean, you think you can figure out who killed Mr. O'Neill? Get real."

"I've solved mysteries before," I said. Guessing the culprit in a children's book totally counts as solving a mystery, right?

"I doubt it. More like, you're trying to find a way to pin the crime on me. I'm not gonna help you with that."

An uncooperative witness! I decided to apply pressure on her, to get her to crack. "So you refuse to talk? You know how suspicious that makes you look?"

"You know how desperate that makes *you* look? Seriously, old man, take care of your baby and leave me alone."

Shoot. So much for applying pressure. I'd be lucky if she ever talked to me again. Still, is it just me, or was she being overly defensive? Maybe she had something to hide.

"Is it true that you waited three minutes before reporting the crime?" I asked.

"Is it true that you're so ugly, you wear your baby's diapers on your face?"

Wow. Harsh, much? "Did you notice anything unusual about the crime scene?"

"I saw a hideous-looking ogre on Mr. O'Neill's computer screen. It must have been a picture of your wife."

"How do you know I'm married?"

"Lucky guess. Is it true you once put a pig in a dress and took it to the company picnic?"

"Okay, now you're just being ridiculous."

"*You're* the ridiculous one, if you think you can accuse me of murder," Natalie said. She tightened her clenched fists. "I'm taking five courses right now. I do *not* have time for police drama."

Mentioning her schoolwork only seemed to make her more upset. "Did you have to skip a class to come here?" I guessed.

"Yes! I tried telling that stupid officer how much I'm paying for tuition, but he didn't care. 'Show up at two, or I'll arrest you!' Please! If he was *going* to arrest me, he would have done it already and saved me from having to work on my macroeconomics project."

"Maybe I can help you with your project," I offered. I figured buttering her up couldn't hurt.

"We have to do the project by ourselves," Natalie said. "Besides, you have a baby. When are you going to get the free time to do college work?"

"Just trying to be nice to a co-worker."

Natalie looked at me suspiciously. "I'd like to believe that, but if you're anything like my roommate, you're just being nice so you can stab me in the back."

"That's not the case. Look, I'm not saying we have to be best friends or anything. I'm just saying, if you help me solve this case, I can clear both of our names."

"No one has accused me of killing Mr. O'Neill," Natalie said.

"Not yet," a dry voice said.

I looked up to see that Detective Dodd had entered, when we weren't paying attention. "How nice to see my two favorite suspects, getting along," he said.

"You'd better have a good reason for bringing me here," Natalie said.

"I do. I'll tell you, once everyone is here."

"Tell me *now*, or I'm going to leave immediately."

Dodd raised his eyebrows at her. "Are you serious?" he asked dangerously.

"Seriously ticked. You police officers are such jerks, thinking you can do whatever you want without any—"

"That's more than enough," Dodd interrupted. "Don't make me arrest you. It'd be a very sad follow-up to clearing you of all charges."

"Clearing me?"

"The autopsy results say the victim died around 4:20 p.m. Since neither of you were around at the time, it clears you of all suspicion."

I smiled. Now *that* was good news.

Natalie smiled too, for about half a second. "Great. Now let me go," she said.

111

"Not so fast," Dodd said. "I took the liberty of arranging a meeting with everyone on your work team. Miss Chang agrees with me that attendance is...mandatory."

Natalie huffed and muttered something about how the entire thing was a waste of time, and Dodd should have just texted her the info. Dodd either didn't hear her, or pretended not to, as he walked over the security desk. "Everything ready?" he asked Barry.

"Yes, sir," Barry said. "You'll be in the Willamette Conference Room. Kelly should already be there."

"Excellent. Lead the way."

Barry led all of us to the Willamette Conference Room, even though Natalie and I already knew where it was. It's at the far end of a hallway, decorated with framed nature photographs. The pictures are sort of generic, except for the one of the Willamette River, and that's only because some prankster had stuck dolphin stickers all over it.

As we reached the end of the hall, I heard a familiar, irritating voice coming from the room.

"And so the guy says to the priest, 'That's not a consubstantial union; *that's my wife!*'"

"Who's the guy with the heavy nasal voice?" Natalie whispered to me.

"Alan," I said. "By the sound of it, his jokes are getting worse." Also, theologically inaccurate.

Barry held the door open, as we all entered. The Willamette Conference room is where we normally have group meetings. There's a whiteboard that doubles as a projection screen on one end, and on the other end are three tables shoved together. Everyone sits in the chairs that surround the table. Alan was already sitting in a chair, talking to a bored-looking Kelly.

Alan turned and smiled as we entered the room. "Not bad for a Thursday!" he said. "Ned, Natalie, I didn't know the meeting would have—wait. You're the officer who talked to me the other day. What's wrong? Did something else happen? Please tell me you're only here because of something tame like a parking violation!"

"I'm here to discuss the murder investigation," Dodd said.

Alan's face fell. "And here I was hoping for an impromptu office party..." he muttered.

Barry shut the door securely, so no one from the outside could overhear, then he took the seat next to Kelly. Natalie and I sat down opposite of them, and Dodd took the seat near the whiteboard, where everyone could easily see him. It was the same seat Mr. O'Neill always used, back when he was alive.

"Good. Now that everyone is here, we can talk about the case," Dodd began.

# Chapter 12

I felt a twinge of excitement go through my body. In mystery books, whenever the detective calls all the suspects together, it's because they're going to review the case and reveal the culprit's identity. It was a sure thing which always happened, without fail!

Unless, of course, the book had thirty pages left, in which case, there was usually a second culprit or a fakeout mystery solution.

"I think I'll begin by discussing the timeline of the case," Dodd said. Internally, I cheered. This was so awesome! "Unless the murderer would like to save us all some time by confessing right now?"

We all looked uneasily at each other. No one said anything, except McKenzie, who was seated on my lap. She said, "Aaa."

Dodd looked like he was going to say something about her, but then he appeared to change his mind. "Fine. Here's the timeline, then. Neil O'Neill arrives at the office in the morning at 8:15, yelling at someone on his cell phone. He tells his assistant Kelly Chang that he will be busy all day, and she is not to disturb him unless it's an emergency."

"He said he was dealing with foreign clients," Kelly said.

"According to the phone records, he *was* on the phone for four hours straight, but not with foreign clients. He was calling various accounting firms in New York. He also called his aunt in Yonkers, but that's hardly relevant to the case. The phone calls end at 11:23 a.m., when he had lunch."

"He didn't leave his office to get lunch," Kelly said.

"Correct. He brought his lunch with him and ate in his office. I'm told he did that often."

"It must be!" Alan said. "I've never seen him in the lunch room! I always figured he had a food allergy, like he was *allergic* to eating with his employees! Ha!"

"I've never seen him in the lunch room either," Barry said.

114

"Let's assume he had lunch from 11:30 to 12:30, then," Dodd said. "Once lunch was over, he went through his email. He sent eight emails, most of them follow-up messages about the phone calls he made. The last email he sent was at 12:55. Then, there's a gap in the timeline where we have no idea what he did."

"I do," Kelly said.

Dodd looked at her intently. "You do? What did O'Neill do at 12:55?"

"He left his office to go to the bathroom."

"For fifteen minutes?" Dodd asked. "Are you sure?"

Kelly turned red. "I don't know how long it takes for him to use the bathroom!" she said defensively. "I just know he left his office and headed towards the restrooms around 1:00."

"That makes sense," Dodd said, nodding slightly. "If you're correct, this is the only time he left the office all day. It's reasonable to assume he was using the facilities."

"You kept track of his bathroom breaks? That's gross," Alan said. "Does anyone else think that's gross? I knew murder investigations were icky, but not in *that* way."

"*Anyway*," Dodd continued, "at 1:07 p.m., Ned Gray is dropped off at the closest bus stop. Gray goes directly to O'Neill's office. Chang tells him to stay out, but Gray insists on going in."

I wanted to object. When he put it that way, it made me sound suspicious. But since he had already told me I was in the clear, I didn't see much point in arguing over it.

"Gray tells O'Neill that he's quitting his job, effective immediately. O'Neill throws a fit, and the two men argue until O'Neill calls security. Security Guard Barry Wells arrives three minutes later and escorts Gray out of the building. O'Neill taunts Gray as he leaves the room, and he locks the door behind him."

"Since he was still alive when I left, that means I didn't kill him," I felt compelled to say.

"After Gray leaves, O'Neill sends an email to his boss, demanding Gray's instant dismissal. At 2:43, O'Neill gets a response, giving him the go-ahead for firing Gray. He immediately sends Chang an email, asking for her to send him the dismissal paperwork. She prints it out on the printer in his office. He sends her another email, saying he'll sign it and give it back to her by the end of the day."

"How do you know this? Were you snooping through the boss' emails?" Alan asked. "What about his right to privacy?"

"I'm trying to solve a murder here," Dodd said dryly. "And emails have timestamps. I'd be an idiot if I didn't make use of them."

"Still doesn't seem fair to me..." Alan muttered.

Dodd ignored him and said, "Here's where it gets interesting. Chang leaves for a half-hour break around 4:05. Both Wells and Alan Stacker take a fifteen minute break at 4:15. And according to the autopsy report, the victim was murdered at 4:20."

At this point, all three of them interrupted Detective Dodd, claiming they were innocent (Kelly), protesting the time that the break started (Barry) and saying that he couldn't make any statements without calling his cousin who was a lawyer that once wrote a speech for a famous celebrity who didn't read the speech word-for-word, but it was still close enough, so it counted (Alan, of course).

Dodd had to call for silence, and it took a minute before they all settled down. Next to me, Natalie made a sarcastic comment about how glad she was she didn't work the same shift as everyone else.

"Like I said, the victim was killed at 4:20," Dodd said. "As you have clearly noticed, everyone was on break when the murder occurred, and no one has an alibi. No one except Gray and Natalie Rose, and that's because they weren't in the building then.

"The murderer arrives at the office. Since the office was locked, either the murderer had a key, or they knocked on the door, and the victim let them inside. Presumably, the two of them talk for a while, before the murderer grabs the three-hole punch from O'Neill's desk and beats him over the head with it. Two, possibly three blows, according to the autopsy.

116

"O'Neill collapsed instead of fighting back, and he died quickly. The murderer wipes their fingerprints off of the weapon, probably using a tissue from the box on O'Neill's desk. They drop the weapon on the ground next to O'Neill, then they leave. Depending on how efficient our murderer is, this could have taken anywhere from one to five minutes.

"The murderer leaves the office at this point, taking the bloody tissue with them. They even lock the door behind them as they go, in order to prolong the body being discovered. By the time everyone's breaks are over, nobody suspects anything is wrong. Stacker leaves work at 5:00. Chang is supposed to leave at 5:00, too, but she stays behind. She's still waiting for O'Neill to give her the paperwork that he promised. Rose comes in to work after 5:00."

"More like 5:10," Natalie said. "The bus was running late. Rush hour traffic, you know."

"Rose comes in to work, checks her email. An email from O'Neill drives her into a fit of rage. She rushes to his office to demand an explanation, before he goes home for the day."

"What made you so mad?" Barry asked.

"I'd rather not say," Natalie said.

"You know how suspicious it looks when you withhold information in a murder investigation?" Barry asked.

"She's not withholding information," Detective Dodd said. "She showed *me* the email. If she chooses not to share it with you, that's her business."

Natalie smirked triumphantly.

"Rose tries opening the door, but it's locked," Dodd said. "So she has Chang unlock the door for her. Rose goes inside, and it takes her approximately forty seconds to discover the body. She screams for Chang to—"

"Forty seconds? I heard it was three minutes," Alan said.

"You heard wrong," Natalie said. "Maybe you should spend more time doing your job, and less time messing around with—"

117

"That's enough. Chang confirmed it was less than a minute," Dodd said. Kelly nodded in agreement. "Rose calls for help. Chang comes in, and together, they call security. They stand outside the door to the room, until Wells arrives. He secures the crime scene and guards it until the police arrive."

"I made sure nobody went in and disturbed the evidence," Barry said.

"A commendable effort, Mr. Wells," Detective Dodd said. "But perhaps too little, too late. The murderer took two things with them when they left the crime scene: the bloody tissue and the paperwork."

"Paperwork?"

"The paperwork for Gray's dismissal. Signed and dated by the late victim himself. Now why would the culprit want to take those papers? Perhaps a vital piece of evidence fell on them? Or perhaps they wanted to frame everyone's favorite diaper daddy."

Diaper jokes? Talk about predictable. "I prefer the term 'stay-at-home dad', thanks," I said sarcastically, as I moved McKenzie from my right arm to my left.

Kelly looked at me. "Are you sure you should have your baby here for this?"

"She can't understand anything that's being said," I said, shrugging. "Besides, there's no one else to watch her."

"Gray," Detective Dodd said. "You're the one who reads mystery books. Did you notice the problem with the evidence?"

"Besides the fact that it's inconclusive?"

Dodd scowled. "The signed papers, Gray. They were removed from the crime scene."

I thought for a moment. "How do you know they were signed, if they weren't at the crime scene?"

"Exactly," Dodd said. "The papers were found in the wastebasket in the front area, where Wells works."

"Hey, I didn't touch those papers," Barry said. "Why would I do something like that? The culprit must be trying to frame me."

"I find it interesting that the culprit would steal paperwork to frame Gray, then try to frame Wells with the same paperwork," Dodd said. "Why not leave the paperwork in Gray's cubicle, to complete the ruse? Why switch halfway through? Is our culprit incompetent, or just desperate to pin the blame on anyone else?"

"Did you fingerprint the paperwork?" I asked.

"Of course," Dodd said. "There were no fingerprints, besides the victim's. Our culprit must have used a tissue again. Or they were wearing gloves. Not all too unusual for winter in Portland, even though it hasn't snowed this month."

If the culprit knew enough to hide their fingerprints, I doubted they were incompetent. Although knowing how incompetent my co-workers usually were, I couldn't be sure.

"We also fingerprinted the door to the victim's office," Dodd said. "Every single one of you touched it that day."

"Whoa! That's not true," Alan said. "I never went inside O'Neill's office!"

"Care to explain how your prints got on the door handle, then?" Dodd asked.

"They must be left over from yesterday!" Alan said. "I'm not a killer! Except when I sing karaoke, ha ha!"

"Nice try, but the cleaning crew wiped the door clean the previous night," Dodd said. "You touched the victim's door on the day of the murder, Mr. Stacker. Why?"

"I...okay, I admit it," Alan said. "I went to see the boss. I wanted to ask him if it was true that Ned was fired. The door was locked, and I never went inside, okay?"

"Why didn't you tell anyone about this?" Barry asked.

"I didn't want to be accused of murder, okay?!" Alan said.

"When did this happen?" Kelly asked. "I don't remember seeing you."

"A little after four," Alan said. "I knew you wouldn't let me into the office to ask about gossip, so I waited for you to go on your break before I went. When I couldn't get in, I went back to my own desk and screwed around until it was time for my own break. That's all."

"It's against the rules to purposely waste time before you go on your break," Kelly said. "That's cheating the company into giving you a double break. I'll have to write you up for that, Alan."

"No!" Alan said. "It was, uh, extenuating circumstances!"

"You just said you were going to gossip with the boss about Ned's firing," Kelly said. "That's hardly extenuating circumstances. And how did you hear that gossip in the first place? Did you take *another* break between one and four?"

"It came up during normal office communications, I swear," Alan said. "I don't use the instant message system to spread rumors! Maybe *hear* rumors, but never spread them!"

"Those are *both* against the rules," Kelly said. "Keep trying to argue against it, and maybe I'll write you up twice."

"No no no no no," Alan said. "If you give me a chance, I can explain. See, I was talking with HR—that's 'HR' as in 'Human Resources', not 'Henry Rackham', although he once told me he wanted to work for HR—"

"Is this real life right now?" Natalie asked. "Because I swear, I've met more mature people in middle school. Grow up, dude."

Detective Dodd cleared his throat. "While I'm enjoying this little display of office politics, we need to get back on track. Stacker, I already have your statement about what happened during your break. I'm going to need a new statement, which says exactly when and *why* you touched the victim's door on Monday. I'll be sure to check your communications from that day, to see if they line up with your story."

"Uh...uh...sure," he said. "Just don't read the private ones."

"I'll be reading *all* of them," Dodd said. "And your emails, too, if you sent any."

120

Alan broke out into a sweat. "You don't need to see what I wrote to my mom," he protested.

"You sent emails to your mother on company time?!" Kelly snapped. "That's against the rules!"

"I wrote it when I was on break!" Alan said.

"Luckily, the timestamp on the email will let us know whether or not you're telling the truth," Dodd said dryly. "As for you, Ms. Chang, now that we know the murder took place during your break, it looks like I *will* have to examine your phone."

"I figured as much," Kelly sighed. She pulled her phone out of her pocket and slid it across the table. "I didn't delete anything, so it should still show that I called my boyfriend."

"You want my phone, too?" Barry said. "I used it on my break, but I didn't make any calls."

"Yes, I'll want the tech guys to examine it, too," Dodd said. Barry got up and handed his phone to the detective, instead of sliding it across like Kelly did.

"What were you doing on your phone, if you weren't calling someone?" Natalie asked. "Were you playing games or texting or something?"

"Nah. I went into the break room and watched a video on my phone," Barry said.

That sounded like a reasonable way to spend your break. "Was it one of my videos?" I asked hopefully.

"Uh, no. Sorry, man."

"Wait. You actually *do* make videos?" Natalie asked. "I thought that was a joke!"

"I do book reviews for the Harvey Brothers series," I said.

"Is that anything like the book reviews that Deirdre Simmons does for the Francy Droo series?" Natalie asked. "Her stuff is awesome."

I frowned. *Thanks for the reminder that Deirdre's videos are more popular than mine, Natalie*, I thought.

"You only watched the one video, correct?" Dodd asked.

"Yeah, it was highlights from last night's basketball game," Barry said.

"He could have left the video running in the background to give himself an alibi, while he committed murder," I pointed out.

"Why would you say that? I thought we were friends," Barry said.

"Just trying to help the investigation," I said.

"I appreciate the enthusiasm, but I'd prefer it if you left the police work to me," Dodd said. "You'll notice *I* don't butt in and criticize you when you're holding the baby wrong."

"What's wrong with the way I'm holding my baby?" I asked.

"You're not supporting her head enough. She could break her neck."

I looked down at McKenzie. I was about to argue that I was holding her in the ideal position for strengthening her neck muscles, but I remembered I didn't want to get arrested for arguing with an officer about the best way to hold a baby. I settled for discretely readjusting her.

Dodd leaned back in his chair. "I think that covers just about everything. I'll have your phones analyzed right away and get back to you by tomorrow. Now if you all will excuse me, I have to take Stacker's statement."

"You're letting us go?" I asked.

"For now," he said ominously.

At the time, I brushed off his comment as a weird quip, but looking back on it, I wonder if Detective Dodd had any idea what was going to happen. Because as it turned out, I *would* see him again. I would see him again, that very same night.

## Chapter 13

When I got back home, I decided to impress my wife by cleaning up a little bit. Nothing too fancy. I mostly just threw out the used diapers, which I had arranged into a smiley face. I thought it was cute, but Brittany would probably disagree.

The counter was still dirty after that, so I wiped it down. I thought about sweeping and mopping the floor, but I decided against it. My day had been busy enough already. Little did I know how busy my night would be!

I checked my phone again to find that I had received five more emails, each one saying another video had been flagged. I tried checking the timestamps like Scott had done, and what do you know? They all got flagged shortly after I left the Mystery Club meeting. This more or less confirmed my suspicion that one of them was the culprit.

But which one was it? I'll be honest, my investigation of them was a total failure. I had gotten a grand total of zero clues from attending their meeting. In fact, I had spent almost the entire time talking about the office murder mystery, not my videos.

I began to suspect this happened on purpose. These people read mysteries all the time. They must know all the good tricks for dodging tough accusations. Clearly, the culprit must have changed the subject on purpose. But which one was the first to change the subject? I couldn't remember.

Well, they weren't the *only* ones who read mysteries. I read them, too. I just had to remember a good detective trick for getting the culprit to reveal themselves. Pretending you already had all the evidence sometimes worked. "Lull the culprit into a false sense of security" was a classic. There was also "trick the culprit into revealing information they couldn't have known otherwise".

Hmmm...that last one seemed promising, especially since I *knew* a piece of information that none of them should have been able to know...

I was distracted when my phone pinged. I picked it up. My wife had just sent me a text message: *Leaving work now. Can't wait to see you!*

"Crap!" I said. "I forgot to make dinner!"

What could I make that would be quick and easy? Sandwiches? Maybe. I didn't remember if we had them last night. What about the leftover cake? No way, that was gone. I had eaten it for lunch. And breakfast. And dessert. Okay, so I ate it for every meal until it was gone. What can I say? Cake is delicious. Even if it's "sorry I ruined your five-year plan cake".

I pulled out some broccoli from the freezer. The instructions said to put it in a microwavable container, add half a cup of water, then cover and cook for six minutes. I found a bowl easily enough, but I didn't know what to cover it with. A paper towel? A dish towel? The dish towel would be nice, because I could use it multiple times, but what if it caught on fire? Do towels catch fire in the microwave?

This is the sort of thing I should have learned in high school. Dish towels and how to do your taxes. Instead, I learned about trigonometry. Lucky me.

I used plastic wrap as a cover and started cooking the broccoli in the microwave. Good. The side dish was taken care of. What about the main course? I rooted around the cupboards and pulled out soup. *That should be easy enough,* I thought. You just dumped soup in a pan and heated in on the stove top until it boiled. I even remembered to put a lid on the pan, so it wouldn't boil over.

That was when I heard the explosion.

I'm not exaggerating. There was a loud popping noise from the microwave, followed by two more. McKenzie started crying, and I picked her up as quickly as I could. With my free hand, opened the microwave door to find the plastic wrap lying on the side of the bowl, not at all doing its job of covering the food. On the top of microwave was a bunch of broccoli bits.

"Did the broccoli explode?" I asked.

"Auh," McKenzie said. I'm pretty sure that was baby talk for "you are undoubtedly correct, my good sir."

124

The broccoli popped, and I jumped backwards, accidentally jostling McKenzie as I did so. I might not be a master chef, but I know that vegetables are not supposed to explode.

Of course, that was when my wife came in. "Hi, Ned!"

"Don't look in the microwave!" I shouted.

"What's wrong with the microwave?"

"Nothing! Just don't look in it!"

Brittany gave me a stern look that cut through to my soul. It contrasted greatly with her nice outfit, which was a dark red turtleneck and work pants. I'm biased, obviously, but I have no idea how anyone could work with Brittany without constantly getting distracted by how sweet she looks. Or maybe I just found her extra attractive that week, because she had spent the last few months in sweat pants and t-shirts. (Please don't get mad at me for revealing your post-birth wardrobe secrets, Brittany.)

"Okay, fine," I said. "I accidentally made the broccoli explode."

Brittany walked over to me and took McKenzie from my arms. "Broccoli doesn't explode. You probably just—Whoa. It *did* explode!"

"Told you!"

"Well, I guess we'll have to have something else for dinner." She kissed me hello.

"I'm also making soup. When do you learn how to do an 'Angry Mom Look'?"

"It's something you learn when you first become a parent. You've got an Angry Dad Look too, you know."

"I do?"

"Sure. Just pretend another baby stepped on McKenzie."

I scowled.

Brittany shook her head. "Angrier. Pretend he also disliked your video channel."

I furrowed my eyebrows and deepened my frown, imitating the angry boy from baby playtime.

"That's it! Good, now you're an official parent. Although it sounds like you already graduated to official status today. Tell me what happened with Jessica. I want to hear *everything*."

I told her what happened earlier that morning. I was just getting to the part when I went back into the playtime room, when the lid to the soup pot started bouncing.

"Uh oh!" I said.

"Quick, turn off the heat!" Brittany said.

I rushed to move the soup, but it was too late. It boiled over the top of the pot and onto the stovetop, where it started sizzling. I turned off the heat and put the soup on a different part of the stove.

"Sorry. I guess I was too wrapped up in my story to pay attention to the soup."

"It's okay. What else do you have ready for dinner?"

"Nothing. Soup and broccoli were going to be it."

Brittany sighed. "I guess we'll have to scavenge for something else."

My eyes lit up. "Can we get pizza?"

"You got pizza earlier this week."

"So?"

Brittany half-laughed. "Being a stay-at-home parent doesn't mean you get to eat pizza for every meal."

"Really? Then why do people have kids?" I wondered.

"It's a mystery."

"I've got more than enough mysteries to solve right now, thanks."

\* \* \*

126

I entered the library at precisely 6:00 p.m. I had a plan, and I was fairly confident of its success. Brittany had agreed with me that this would be the best way to expose my Harvey-hating culprit.

All the other members of the Mystery Club were in the conference room, when I arrived. They were back to wearing normal clothes, although Fake Frenchman still had his mustache on. I guess it wasn't a fake mustache, after all.

"Ned? You're back?" Deirdre asked.

"Sorry for leaving unexpectedly yesterday," I said. "There was a problem with the baby."

"I thought you ran out on us, because you were too much of a wimp to handle being stabbed to death," Kay said.

Personally, I'd much rather change diapers than get stabbed. Luckily, I'm pretty sure I'll never be forced to make a choice between the two.

"Nope," I said cheerfully. "I love mysteries, and this seems like a great group. What are we all discussing tonight?"

"Thievery," said Sherlock Holmes.

"Awesome," I said. I took a deep breath, then went into full fanboy mode. "That means I pretty much *have* to talk about *Harvey Brothers: The Tower Theft*. It's the first, and best, book in the series. Have any of you read it?"

Everyone shook their heads and said no.

Deirdre took a piece of paper off of the conference table. "Here's our reading list for the month. It's how we make sure everyone's read the same books." She pointed out the section labelled "Thursday". I gave it a glance and saw eight or so books, most of them with "theft" or "robbery" in the title.

"Do you have to read all of them?" I asked.

"No, but it helps if you read at least three of them," Deirdre said. "That way, it's likely more than one person has read it. Here, let me get you the list for next month."

"That's okay! You don't *have* to read multiple books about theft, when you read the Harvey Brothers," I said. "It's so good, you'll never read another mystery again!"

Fake Frenchman snorted. "I doubt that!"

"The story is that an old billionaire died unexpectedly," I said. "All his money was hidden in the property somewhere, but no one knew where."

"That's ridiculous. You can't hide a billion dollars in cash on your property. It'd take up too much room."

"Normally that'd be true, but he was super smart. He was a doctor who taught at a public university. He taught doctor things. I don't know what it meant—I kind of skipped that part—but it sounded like high-level stuff to me."

"That's not—you don't become a billionaire by teaching at a public university!" Fake Frenchman rubbed his forehead and looked at the others for support. "Are we really going to do this? Nobody else has read this insipid book."

"There's no rule saying we can't discuss children's mysteries," Deirdre said. She gave him a look that clearly said "I know he's an idiot. Let's humor him, anyway. We never get new recruits."

"Should be a rule," Kay said. "Not enough violence in kids' stuff. All the blood gets cleaned up."

Sherlock Holmes cleared his throat. "So a large amount of money disappeared. Were there any clues as to its whereabouts?"

"He left a will, but it was all in a secret code," I said. "Numbers for letters! 1 equals A, 2 equals B and so on."

"That's the easiest, most obvious secret code ever," Fake Frenchman huffed.

"But it was locked in a safe, protected by another code!" I said. "That's what made it tricky. And there was a deadline! The Harveys had to find the will within a week, or the property would go to John Jerkley. He was going to kick the widow off the property and turn the entire thing into an ice cream store."

"Ice cream store?" Sherlock Holmes asked.

"A *billionaire* didn't leave any protections for his wife?" Kay asked.

"The culprit's name is *John Jerkley?*" Deirdre asked.

"Ice cream is delicious, I already said his death was unexpected, and that's the most awesome culprit name ever," I said. "The Harveys investigate the property. They notice a shadowy figure dancing around the base of the tower, trying to get in."

"How does *dancing* help you enter a locked tower?" Fake Frenchman asked.

"Not very well, I'd say!" I replied. "The culprit didn't get in. The Harveys go inside the tower themselves, to see if they can find what the culprit was searching for."

"How'd they get in the tower, if it was locked?" Deirdre asked.

"Oh, the key was in the lock the whole time," I said. "John Jerkley didn't notice it, that's all."

The Fake Frenchman groaned.

"So the Harveys climb up the tower, when a werewolf holding a stolen wallet appears," I said. "They chase after the werewolf and retrieve the wallet. The numbers on the driver's license open the victim's safe."

As you can tell, Fake Frenchman was getting angrier and angrier, the longer I spoke. At this point, he finally exploded. "It was a cat, you idiot! It was the victim's cat, and it had the safe combination written on the underside of its collar! There's no werewolves or driver's licenses in the story!"

*Gotcha.* I folded my arms across my chest triumphantly. "How do you know that if you've never read the book?"

Fake Frenchman knew he was cornered, but he didn't give up. "I...I...I read a review of it," he said.

"More like you *saw* a review of it. *My* review," I pointed my finger at him dramatically, which is something I've always wanted to do. "You're the one who flagged my videos. Admit it!"

Fake Frenchman fell to his knees and screamed. "You're right! I flagged them as inappropriate content! I was hoping to get your stupid videos removed from the Internet!"

"Uh, that's crazy harsh," Deirdre said. "Why would you want to get his videos removed?"

*"I hate the Harvey Brothers!"* he shouted. "Dictionary Dan is the best children's mystery series. The Harveys are *nothing* compared to Dan. And yet Dan got cancelled decades ago, while they're still making Harvey books. Why can't they let that pathetic series *die already?!*"

"Literary murder," Kay said. "Reminds me of the book where someone pushed a shelf onto a librarian."

"So you tried to sabotage Ned's reviews because you don't like the Harvey Brothers series," Sherlock Holmes said. "I'm sorry Brian, but that's really pathetic."

"Yeah, being an online troll isn't cool," Deirdre said.

"It wasn't *my* idea. You were the one who showed us Ned's videos, and how to flag them," Fake Frenchman said.

*"What?"* I asked.

"That was just an *example!*" Deirdre said. "I didn't mean you should go ahead and attack Ned's videos. The poor guy gets so few views at it is. Why make it harder for him?"

"Ouch," I said. "Still, I have to—"

"He's going to unflag the videos right away, aren't you, Brian?" Deirdre asked.

"Yes," he said meekly. "I'm sorry. It was nothing personal. I just...I don't like the Harvey Brothers."

"I figured that out, thanks," I said.

Brian left to use one of the library's computers. He came back in a few minutes, announcing that he was done. I checked on my phone, and sure enough, none of my videos were listed as having inappropriate content anymore. I could get my meager ad revenue again. Victory!

\* \* \*

I stuck around for about ten minutes after that, even though I didn't know any of the books they were discussing. One of them called *The Cheeseburger Thefts* sounded interesting, though. I made a mental note to check it out, whenever I got the chance.

Once the group took a break, I cornered Deirdre. As far as I was concerned, the entire situation was her fault.

"You taught that jerk how to flag my videos," I said. "Do you know how much trouble you caused?"

"I didn't do it on purpose," Deirdre said. "Give me a break."

"No way! If it wasn't for you, he never would have bothered me. You *owe* me for this."

Deirdre sighed and adjusted her hair clip. "Fine, you're right. I'll help you prove your innocence to the police."

"Wait, really?" I asked. "Gosh, I was just going to ask you to collaborate with me on a *Francy Droo and Harvey Brothers Super Mystery* review."

"Ooo, let's do that instead," Deirdre said quickly.

"Too late!" I said. "What's this about proving my innocence?"

"I was thinking about it, when you told us about the murder at yesterday's meeting. I've read just as many mysteries as you have, you know. I know *exactly* what to do in situations like this..."

## Chapter 14

That night at 7:30, I got up to leave the house. I was hoping to leave without being noticed, but Brittany caught me at the door.

"You're going out again?" she asked. "Didn't you just get back from the Mystery Club?"

"Yes, but, uh...I'm going out drinking with the guys," I said. "I don't know when I'll be back, so—"

"But you don't drink, and you don't have any guy friends besides the pizza guy."

"Did I say I was going out drinking with the guys? I meant to say, I'm going to watch the big game. By myself."

Brittany shook her head. "You're not very good at lying. Where are you *really* going?"

"I...I can't say. I don't want you to worry."

"In other words, you're about to do something incredibly stupid that's going to make me furious with you."

"Pretty much," I admitted. Dang. How did she know me so well?

Brittany was clearly unhappy with me. "Give me one good reason why I should let you go."

"I'll take the baby with me, so you can have a night alone."

"Deal!" Brittany said. She threw the diaper bag at me. "Don't hurry back!"

Wow. She was so eager to get rid of me, I was almost insulted. How long had it been since she had a night to herself? A long time, I realized. As in...I dunno, probably before the baby was born.

"What happened to being worried about me?" I asked.

"You can't get in *that* much trouble if you're going somewhere you can bring the baby," she said.

132

* * *

A half hour later, I was at my office building, ready to start the mission. Deirdre's plan was relatively simple. I would sneak into Mr. O'Neill's office and search for evidence. There had to be something that the culprit had missed, some clue that the police overlooked because it didn't make sense to them.

Believe it or not, Deirdre was wearing a bright pink feather boa. She had a short green skirt which matched her fedora. And here, I thought detective costume night was yesterday.

"You brought the baby with you?" Deirdre asked, wrinkling her nose at me. "Why'd you do that?"

"My wife wouldn't let me out of the house without her," I said.

"Hmph. What part of *top secret mission* didn't you understand? That means *no baby-sitting.*"

"She's going to fall asleep in a few seconds." It was true. McKenzie's eyes were closing after the long car ride. "Besides, it's not like I'm bringing her into the building with me. We'll just leave her in the car while we go in. She'll be fine for a few minutes by herself."

"Okay, number one, you are the worst parent ever, for saying that," Deirdre said. "Number two, I'm not going in there."

"But you said you would distract the security guard!"

Deirdre rolled her eyes. "Do you ever pay attention? I said I would get the perfect distraction. I didn't say I would *be* a distraction! No way am I getting caught if you screw this up."

"You confidence in me is inspiring," I deadpanned.

"Whatever. Here's your earpiece." Deirdre pulled back her hair, revealing that she was wearing two earpieces. You know, the things you use to have hands-free phone conversations while driving? She took off the left one and gave it to me. "I synced them together. This way, I can be in contact with you, even though I won't be in the building. I'll warn you if anything bad happens."

"Can I get one that *wasn't* just in your ear?"

"No, and this mission is going to be a failure unless you start being more observant."

"What do you—?"

"Hello," a voice behind me said.

I shrieked, and Deirdre smirked at me. "Observant people don't get snuck up on."

"That's not—" I began to say. Then I saw our guest was none other than Movie Star Mom. This time, the nickname fit. She was wearing a full-length blue dress that sparkled as she moved and hugged her body like a toddler with a teddy bear. Her hair flowed more smoothly than the ocean, her makeup highlighted her cheeks, and I could swear that her face was glowing.

In other words, she was drop-dead gorgeous that night. All thoughts left my mind, and all I could say was, "Guh..."

"Sorry I'm late," Movie Star Mom said. "I had trouble finding the place."

"No worries," Deirdre said. "Nice distraction outfit."

I tore my eyes away from Movie Star Mom to look at Deirdre. "Wait. *She's* the distraction?"

Deirdre made an annoyed sound. "Based on the way you were ogling her just now, I'd say she makes a *perfect* distraction!"

"I was *not* ogling her! I wasn't, I swear. I don't even know your name."

"Melancthea," she said.

Mel the Movie Star. Of course.

"And just *how* do you two know each other?"

"She's my hair stylist," Mel said. "You think my hair looks like this normally? No, Deirdre is a hair wizard!"

"Thank you," Deirdre said. "You told us that the security guard is desperate for a girlfriend, right? I'm sure he'll be *very* interested in her. Unless you'd rather dress up in a wig and flirt with him yourself?"

"Mel will do just fine," I said quickly.

"I'm not sure I'm comfortable flirting with a man who's not my husband, even if it's for a good cause," Mel said. "I figured I could pose as a lost tourist, instead. I even brought a map, see?" She unfolded it and held it out. "Large enough to block the security guard's view!"

"Good idea," Deirdre said. "Mel, you can go in first. When it's safe, Ned will follow."

"And what will you do?"

"I'll stay on guard here, and I'll let the two of you know if there are any problems," Deirdre said. She removed the other earpiece from her ear and handed it to Mel. "Here, wear this so you can keep in contact with us."

"You're also going to watch the baby, right, Deeds?" I asked.

"Don't ever call me that," Deirdre said.

Mel looked down, noticing McKenzie for the first time. "You brought your baby with you on a spy mission?"

"*Thank you*," Deirdre said. "I told him he was being stupid."

"I couldn't get out of the house, unless I brought her with," I said. "Besides, McKenzie is a wonderful baby who won't screw things up like the one baby did in *Harvey Brothers #127: The Kidnapped Baby-Sitters*."

"What are you even talking about?" Mel asked.

"We're doomed," Deirdre said. "We are so, so doomed. You're going to ruin the plan."

"But the plan was *your* idea!" I protested.

"Look, I'm just saying if you get arrested, it's not my fault," she said.

"I won't get arrested. What's the worst that can happen? I search the office and find no evidence at all?"

"That's *probably* what's going to happen, but worst case scenario is that the security guard shoots you, and you die."

"Gee, thanks."

"What are ex-girlfriends for?" Deirdre said, smiling sweetly at me.

"Well, if we're going to be grim about this..." I said. I took a deep breath and prepared a heroic goodbye speech. "If I don't make it out of here alive, tell my wife I love her. Make sure McKenzie is taken care of. Also, be nice to Scott when I'm gone."

"The pizza guy? What are you talking about?" Deidre asked.

"He's got a crush on you."

"Aw, that's cute!" Mel said. "Deirdre's always complaining how guys say no whenever she asks them out. I tried loaning her some of my clothes to help, but it didn't work. I think men are intimidated by her—"

"We are *not* discussing my dating issues right now!" Deirdre said. I made a mental note to continue the conversation with Mel another time. The story of Deirdre Simmons' failed love life sounded *good*.

\* \* \*

Mel went into the building first. She went straight to the security desk and started talking to Barry. He seemed *very* interested in what she had to say. Like Deirdre had thought, Mel was the perfect distraction.

After thirty seconds, I followed her into the building. Mel had left the door partially open on purpose, so I didn't have to worry about making any noise while I opened the door. I still had to avoid Barry's line of sight though, so I crawled across the floor instead of walking at eye level.

"You look like an idiot," Deirdre said, her voice coming through in my earpiece. "She's holding the map in front of the guard's face now. Hurry!"

I snuck past the guard station, to the doors that led to the main building. It was the moment of truth. I pulled out my employee ID card and slid it through the reader, praying it would still work.

One second. Two seconds. Then the light turned green, as the door unlocked.

I tapped my earpiece and whispered, "I'm in."

"Great. Melancthea, he's in. Wrap it up, if you can. We don't—ow! Your stupid baby pulled my boa! I told you babies don't work on secret missions!"

Mel giggled loudly. "I *know*." I figured that was her way of acknowledging what Deirdre had just said. She asked Barry another question, as I rolled through the doorway. That's *one* advantage to having an infant. You're so used to being down on your hands and knees all the time, it's easy to move around during covert operations.

I quickly dodged left, to be out of sight of the door I had just gone through, then I stood up. Nobody else was around. Good. I hadn't expected anyone to be there, since most of the night crew works on the other side of the building.

I hurried towards the area with my cubicle and Mr. O'Neill's office. Just in time, I realized that there was a light coming out of the cube on the end.

"Hello?" a voice asked. I recognized it as Natalie's. "Someone there?"

I ducked behind a wall as Natalie leaned out of her cube. Shoot! Why didn't I think of that? Of *course* she would work somewhere close to me, if we had the same boss! I had walked by her cube a hundred times during the day, but I had never put two and two together and realize it belonged to someone on the night shift.

"You okay?" Deirdre asked.

"Shhhh!" I said. I didn't need any distractions.

"If this is a joke, it's not funny," Natalie warned. "God, people are so stupid." She huffed and went back into her cube.

It was a lucky break for me, but I didn't believe in taking chances. I'd have to take the long way around. I went over two cubicles, and crap. At the end of the hall, there was a light on in the CFO's office. That didn't mean she was *there*, of course. She could have just left it on when she went home for the night. Still, was it worth risking it?

137

"Ned, Melancthea's out of the building," Deirdre said. "We'll send her back in when you need to get out. Are you in the office yet?"

"I'm trying to find the right route," I whispered, tapping my earpiece. "One of my co-workers is here, and there's a light on in one of the offices."

"You didn't plan the route ahead of time?" Deidre asked.

"No. You didn't tell me to."

"Well, duh, that's because I thought it was obvious. You're the only one who knows the layout of the building, after all."

"Ned, can you hear me?" Mel asked. "I have an important question."

"Yes, I hear you. What is it?"

"Does your baby like stuffed animals? I have one in my purse that I can give her."

"If she's starting to wake up, give her the green dog that's in her diaper bag." I'm pretty sure that's a sentence which has never been used in a spy movie.

"Where's the diaper bag?"

"It's in...oh," I said. I was about to say it was in my car, when I realized it was on my shoulder, as usual. "Never mind. The diaper bag is here with me."

"The bag you brought with you is a *diaper bag?*" Deirdre asked. "I thought that was for fingerprint kits and stuff like that. Who brings a *diaper bag* on a covert mission?"

"I didn't mean to! I guess I just got used to having it with me at all times," I said.

"It's true," Mel said. "I bring mine wherever I go."

"I am never doing a secret mission with stay-at-home parents again," Deirdre said.

"Don't ask me to baby-sit when you and Scott have kids," I said.

138

Deirdre let out an angry groan of frustration, while Mel giggled. I was about to follow up with a hilarious dad joke, when I was caught. Sort of.

"Okay, I heard something" Natalie said. "Stop trying to scare me! Just because there's been a murder, it doesn't mean it's funny to sneak around here at night!"

Startled, I accidentally dropped my earpiece and hid in the nearest cubicle. It was a dumb mistake, but it ended up being a good distraction. When Natalie saw it, she picked it up and stopped searching the area.

"Oh, I see how you've been doing this now," she said. She tapped the side of the earpiece and held it to her mouth.

*"Leave me alone, you idiots!"* she yelled.

Knowing Deirdre, I figured she would make a smart aleck remark like "Wow, Ned, your voice got a lot higher. Did you go through reverse puberty?" But no, I guess Deirdre was smarter than I gave her credit for. She started playing a song on her phone.

Natalie listened for a few seconds, then scoffed. "It was just a stupid radio the whole time," she said. "Phew. I guess I was scaring myself over nothing."

She turned off the earpiece and pocketed it, before going back to her cubicle. Darn. There went my connection to the outside world.

For a moment, I wondered if I should leave. This mission was a bad idea from the start, and now it was getting worse. But then I realized that there was almost no chance of me getting back outside without drawing Barry's attention. Not unless I got Natalie's help. And I couldn't go to her, unless I was sure she wasn't the real killer.

I decided to press on. Maybe I could stop by my cubicle on the way out. Maybe the phone would still work. And maybe I'd still remember Deirdre's phone number? Yeah, right. Like I knew any phone numbers besides mine and my wife's. I'd have to call Brittany, so she could call Deirdre. Embarrassing, but better than being arrested.

Since Natalie seemed to be on high alert, I went down the aisle of cubicles that I was currently in. I tried staying close to the cubicle entrances, so I

139

could duck into one if need be. I stopped to listen when I got close enough to the CFO's office. There was no noise at all coming out of it, not even the hum of a computer. Not that I'd be able to hear a computer running through a closed door, but still. The office was empty.

I turned the corner and walked towards Mr. O'Neill's office. I could smell it, before I could see it; the stench of chemicals was *heavy* in the air. I guess that meant they had tried to clean it. Did that mean the police were done with the office?

Sure enough, there was no longer any police tape covering the door, just a little rope. I figured that meant it wasn't a crime scene anymore. Good. If I got arrested, the charge would be less serious.

*You're not going to get arrested, Ned. Think positive.*

I reached out and slowly turned the handle. The door was unlocked. Despite Natalie discovering my earpiece, it seemed luck was on my side that night. The door made a little bit of noise as I pushed it past the door frame, but after that, it swung in smoothly.

Stepping over the rope, I slipped inside the room and partially closed the door behind me. Time to investigate.

# Chapter 15

*"Looks like you were right, Jim," Fred said. "This old pirate map is real! The 'X' on the map led us straight to this cave!"*

*"Then I guess we'd better X-plore it!" Jim said.*

*"I M-plore you not to make jokes like that!" Fred said.*

*Laughing, the two brothers went into the queer-looking cave. They hadn't made it two steps, before a sword-wielding pirate jumped out at them.*

*"Stay away!" he growled, holding his deadly cutlass to Jim's throat.*

I was glad that there weren't any sword-wielding pirates waiting for me inside Mr. O'Neill's office. No one was there besides me. I reached into my diaper bag and pulled out a small flashlight. It took me a few tries to click it on, since I was wearing gloves. I didn't want to leave fingerprints behind, after all.

First, I examined the visitor's chair, the one that I had been sitting in when Mr. O'Neill chewed me out. It was hard plastic and uncomfortable— O'Neill didn't like visitors. Based on the imprints in the carpet, it was in the same place where it always stood.

I ran my finger along the armrest. There was no dust. There didn't seem to be anything unusual with the seat, either. There was a lever at the bottom which you could use to adjust the height. I tried desperately to remember what height setting it had been at when I used it last, but it was useless. I hadn't looked at that lever, when I talked with Mr. O'Neill. In fact, I barely looked at the chair. I was more focused on the conversation.

The chair was about a foot away from his desk. The culprit couldn't have been sitting down, when they hit O'Neill on the head. It was too far for someone to reach. The culprit must have been standing up and leaning over the desk when they hit O'Neill in the back of the head.

Was O'Neill hit on the back of his head, though? I don't think Detective Dodd specified what part of the head was hit, just that O'Neill had been hit twice. I guess I just assumed that he was facing the opposite of the killer.

That way, he wouldn't see the fatal blow coming. But why would he have his back to a visitor?

I tried leaning over the desk from the front. Yes, there was plenty of room to reach his chair. Even someone a foot smaller than me could hit the back of O'Neill's head, especially if O'Neill was sitting at the time.

The top of the desk had papers smeared all over it randomly, which more or less confirmed that O'Neill had grabbed at his desk before falling to the ground. I picked up one paper and read it. Financial statement. Next one was a spreadsheet. Next one was an email about the possible impact to quarterly earnings if we partnered with another company on some project I had never heard of before.

I put the papers back where I found them. Clearly, this was all normal business stuff. I shouldn't have been surprised. If O'Neill had a paper that indicated the culprit's identity, the culprit probably would have taken it with them when they left the crime scene.

I glanced right. By the computer monitor was the box of tissues. It was the kind where you could remove a tissue, without touching the box. It would have been all too easy for the culprit to take a tissue without leaving fingerprints. I picked up the box. It felt relatively full.

I hit the power button on the monitor, but nothing happened. After a few seconds, a small text box reading "no input" appeared on the screen. Huh. I did a quick look around, and sure enough, there was no computer tower. I guess either the police or the IT department had taken it out of the office.

I tried remembering where his three-hole punch had been. It was the side of his desk, next to his tray for outgoing papers. If you were sitting in the visitor's chair, it would be to your left. Did that mean the culprit was left-handed? Were any of my co-workers left-handed? I didn't know, but it wasn't impossible to grab it with your left hand and flip it to your right hand before attacking.

The papers on the tray had been jostled, compared to the papers on the incoming tray, next to it. Either O'Neill was messy with paperwork he was getting rid of, or the culprit had hit the tray when grabbing the murder weapon.

142

I let out a deep breath. I didn't see anything else I could investigate from this side of the office. It was time to check O'Neill's side of the room.

I went around the desk and waved my flashlight on the ground, expecting to see a chalk outline indicating where the body had been. There wasn't any outline, but there was a dark stain by the foot of the desk. Blood, most likely. That had to have been where his head landed. If he had fallen onto his desk and slipped down to the ground, then yes. He would've landed close to there.

The desk had a set of drawers on the right, like all the desks in our office do. The bottom drawer contained personnel files. There was one for every member of our team, including the ones that weren't suspects in the murder. I noted that someone had crossed out the name on my file with a black marker.

*Why?* I wondered. Could it be that this murder was a deliberate attempt to frame me? Did someone hate me so much, they were willing to kill in order to land me in jail?

No. It was more likely O'Neill had scratched out the name on my file after firing me. I opened up the folder. There was a copy of every performance review I had been given, along with two annual evaluations. Towards the back was a biography, my resume—they *still* had my resume?—and papers which took me a while to recognize as notes from the original interviews I had given. Someone had drawn a doodle of a dinosaur on the side of the notes. Well, *that* was an unwelcome insight into the hiring process.

That was when my flashlight gave out. I hit the side of it, and the light came back on. I had purposely picked a weak flashlight for this mission. I figured if I used a full-powered one, someone from outside the office would be more likely to see it, and I'd be caught.

I quickly flipped through the other folders. They looked the same: mostly performance reviews. Kelly's folder had a black-and-white picture of her, attached to the inside. Someone had scribbled *The Punisher enforces the rules. Keep her around.* on it. I wondered if O'Neill had written that, and why.

Finally, I pulled the top drawer open. Inside was a plastic organizer holding pencils, paperclips, rubber bands and other office supplies. Small pink papers flashed at me from underneath. Sticky notepaper?

My flashlight dimmed, but it still stayed on. I was starting to regret my choice of flashlights.

Looking closer, the pink papers were lottery tickets, ten of them dated Monday. I guess our friend O'Neill played regularly. No wonder the company was having financial problems. One of them had writing on it. I was about to pick it up, when the printer sprang to life.

I instinctively jumped, accidentally knocking the contents of the drawer into my diaper bag. Shoot. I quickly put the plastic container back in the drawer and shut it, before going to the printer. It was a bulky device on a smaller desk in the back, next to a...I think it was a fax machine. I've never used one, so I wouldn't know. The printer was making guttural noises as it spit out a paper.

Who would print something this late at night? Maybe someone had selected the wrong printer by accident. I know I had done that once before, and I got an earful from Mr. O'Neill for my mistake. Curious, I picked up the paper.

*O'Neill—*

*You can't fire me like that! How am I supposed to take care of my family, now? You heartless monster! I'm going to make sure you get exactly what you deserve! Watch your back!*

A threat. There was no name attached, and also, no timestamp. Was this threat recent, or had it been sitting in the queue for the last several days? Maybe turning on the computer monitor had triggered the printer, somehow.

I looked closer at the printer's touchscreen. It listed the ink levels—he had a color printer? No fair!—along with a "print queue" button with the number "3" on it. I tapped the button, when I heard the door open behind me.

I quickly turned around, to find Alan standing there, frowning. "Looking for something, Ned?" he asked, closing the door behind him.

144

"Hi, Alan," I said. "I...uh...I know what this looks like..."

Alan crossed his arms over his chest and arched an eyebrow at me. "It looks like you broke into the office after hours, so you could interfere with the crime scene," he said coolly.

"*Search* the crime scene. I was hoping to find clues about the culprit's identity."

"More like you were hoping to *hide clues* of your *guilt*," Alan said. "Give me one good reason why I shouldn't call security and have you arrested."

I decided to appeal to his better nature. "I'm innocent, I swear! You've got a wife and kid, just like me. You know what it's like. You'd do anything to help protect them! Well, me too. That's why I had to come here to prove I didn't do it."

"Don't talk to me about my family," Alan sneered. "They're the reason I got into this mess in the first place."

"*You're* the killer?" I gasped.

In retrospect, I shouldn't have been surprised. Half of the *Harvey Brothers* books end with a culprit confrontation, even though in real life, every book should end with the sentence "Fred and Jim called the police, and the criminals were arrested".

"I'm the *victim* in all this," Alan said. "My life has been a living nightmare, ever since my wife got pregnant five years ago. She used to be the most wonderful person, laughing at my jokes, telling me how much she loved me. But once she became pregnant? That was the end of it. She got angry and yelled all the time."

I know I should have been paying closer attention to what Alan was saying—after all, I was *trapped in a room with a killer*—but all I could think of was escaping, not chatting. How could I get past him? I couldn't. He was standing in front of a closed door.

"Pregnancy can be difficult, with all the hormones and stuff," I said, trying to stall for time.

"And when the baby was born, it got worse. You stay-at-home parents are the scum of the Earth, you know that? You sit on the couch and do nothing *all day!* How can you spend eight hours at home every day, doing *nothing?* Is it even *possible* to be that lazy? Why can't you get a job like a normal person?"

That was uncalled for. "Hey, being a stay-at-home parent is a lot of work. It's not easy taking care of an infant. There are the diapers, and—"

"Oh yes, the *diapers!* You know what my wife does? Instead of throwing them away, she makes them into little piles. Our entire house has diaper piles everywhere. No matter where I go, I can't escape the *stink!* Why can't you throw them out like normal people? You're so lazy, you'd rather sit in *filth* than get off your butt and clean."

I decided not to comment. Where was security, when you needed it? Was there some way for me to signal Barry for help? There weren't any security cameras in Mr. O'Neill's office, obviously, otherwise his death wouldn't have been a mystery. Was there a security camera in the hall that I could trigger from inside the room?

"The house is a mess all the time. 'I'm too busy to clean,' she says. Busy doing what? Not preparing dinner, that's for sure! Ever since the baby was born, Roberta's cooking has been a disaster! You know she managed to burn soup yesterday? *She burned the soup!* How do you even *do* that? And now that she's pregnant *again*, things are only going to get worse!"

Alan had raised his voice at the mention of his wife's pregnancy, which gave me an idea. What if I purposely got him mad? That would be dangerous, obviously, but maybe he would start shouting, and Natalie would notice. She could come in and save me.

"Whatever," I said. "You're just being a loser. Get a life."

Alan's eyes almost popped out of his head. "Don't you *dare* defend her! I know you've been cozying up to her at that stupid baby playtime! She wouldn't shut up about how great you were when I got home today! What man wants to hear his wife extol the virtues of a loser like you?!"

Baby playtime? There was no Roberta in...oh my gosh! Alan was married to *Sleeping Woman?*

"That's your *wife?!*" I asked.

146

"Don't play dumb. You've probably been flirting with *all* the women at the playtime. That's the *real* reason you became a stay-at-home dad, isn't it? You're some kind of creepy predator."

"That is so untrue, I don't even know how to address it."

"Deny it all you want, but you're a weirdo and a creep, and I'm *glad* I'm framing you for O'Neill's murder."

That sounded like a confession. "So you *are* the murderer."

"That's right," Alan admitted. "My life at home has been awful, and it's not much better, here at work. O'Neill is always yelling at me, threatening to fire me. You don't know this, but he was laughing when he came into the office that morning. He bragged that he had the perfect solution to the company's money problems. When I asked him what it was, he just laughed at me. But I could see it sticking out of his folder—a pink slip! I just knew he was going to give me the boot!"

"So he *was* planning to fire someone this week..." I said. He had basically said as much, when he fired me. "But how do you know he was going to fire *you?* He threatened to fire *everyone* at one point or another. Maybe he was planning to fire Natalie, because she has the least seniority."

"You think O'Neill cared about *seniority?* He'd fire us both in an *instant* and replace us with unpaid interns, if he could get away with it. I'm telling you, I *saw* him taking a pink slip into his office."

"And you panicked, because you assumed you would be fired," I deduced.

"As soon as I saw Kelly leave, I went into O'Neill's office to beg for my job. When I saw the paperwork on his desk, labelled 'Termination of Employment'? And it was *signed?* I couldn't think clearly. I grabbed the three-hole punch and smashed him over the head with it. I didn't mean to *kill* him, I just—I just wanted to show him I was serious!"

That didn't sound right to me. "You thought you could hit him on the head with a three-hole punch, and what? He'd give you your job back? Why would he let you stay with the company, after you attacked him? He wasn't the type to forgive and forget."

"Okay, so maybe I *did* want to kill him," Alan said. He pushed his glasses up his nose. "I told you, I wasn't thinking clearly. My body was moving of its own accord! When I realized what I had done, I used a tissue to clean the weapon and take the paperwork. It wasn't until later that I noticed *your* name was on it, not mine."

Well, that explained why my resignation paper had been removed from the office. I cast a glance at the clock. I had been inside the building for over ten minutes. Where was Deirdre? Where was Mel? Surely they had gone for help by now?

"If you're the killer, that doesn't explain what you're doing here tonight," I said. "The murder was days ago."

"Yeah, but the officer with the dumb name was giving me a hard time *today*. I decided to end the investigation early by printing out an incriminating paper in O'Neill's office. I did it from *your* computer, of course."

"You don't know my password."

"It's 'LoveBrittany'. How corny can you get?" Alan sneered. "I was *going* to make it seem like the threat from you didn't print out until just now, because the printer was off. And that would be it. Kelly would find the threat, you'd be arrested, I'd get your job and walk away free."

Alan grinned at me. "Everyone thinks I'm a harmless idiot, but I'm smarter than you think. That act I put on in the supply room, pretending I didn't know how three-hole punches work? That sure took me off your suspect list, quick. You fell for my trick like the idiot you are."

"Yes, you fooled me," I admitted. "So what now?"

Alan shrugged. "I'm not sure. You ruined my plans by showing up here tonight, but that's not bad. For *me*, at least. I don't have to tell *you* how guilty you look, breaking in here at night with an incriminating paper."

"I'll tell the police everything you just told me," I said.

"Who's going to believe you? You're the ex-employee with an axe to grind," Alan laughed. "But...if you're not going to go quietly...maybe I should kill you now!"

148

Uh oh. A death threat. I was fairly certain I could take Alan on in a fistfight—he didn't look like he had exercised at all in the past ten years—but I didn't want to push my luck against someone who could kill a man with office supplies.

What would the Harvey Brothers do in this situation? They'd find a way to stop the culprit from a distance. Like...throwing something at him!

I sneaked a hand into my diaper bag and grabbed the flashlight.

"Maybe this will *illuminate the truth!*" I shouted, throwing the flashlight at Alan's head.

Alan dodged, and the flashlight fell harmlessly against the door. "Seriously? You thought you could knock me out with a flashlight?"

Crap. I missed. *That* never happened in the *Harvey Brothers* books.

"Say goodnight, Ned," Alan grinned. He stretched his hands towards me, walking around the desk. Desperately, I grabbed the first thing in my diaper bag. A baby bottle!

"Eat formula!" I shouted, twisting off the cap and throwing the expired formula into Alan's face. He screamed and grabbed at his eyes. I dropped the diaper bag and quickly ran past him, yanking open the door.

"Oh no you don't!" He lunged for me. I dodged by rolling on the ground, out of the office. Suddenly, I was *so glad* we did rolling games at baby playtime. The less coordinated Alan smashed into the door. "Ow! I'll kill you for this!"

I was already running down the aisle. "Natalie! Call security! Alan is the killer!"

Natalie leaned out of her cubicle. "What are you—what?"

Alan screamed in anger and started running after me.

"Just get security!" I yelled.

"On it!" Natalie said.

Alan jumped for the entrance to Natalie's cubicle, but he missed and fell flat on his stomach. He didn't get up after that.

149

"Can't get up? You should do tummy time more often," I suggested.

"This never would have happened on a Favorite Day Friday..." he groaned.

# Chapter 16

I sat on Alan, preventing him from getting back up. He started blubbering, and at one point, he tried scratching my legs. Fortunately, it wasn't too long before Barry arrived and slapped a pair of handcuffs on him.

I followed Barry, as he dragged Alan back to the front office area. Deirdre and Mel were both there, standing by Barry's desk. Deirdre was holding McKenzie, who was yanking on her clothes. So they *had* tried to rescue me! I appreciated their efforts. I probably would have appreciated them more, if they had actually succeeded.

"You're alive!" Deirdre said.

"And you caught the real culprit?" Mel asked.

"Sure did!" I said.

"Good for you," Deirdre said, "because your baby needs a diaper change, and there is *no way* that I'm doing it."

I walked over to them and took McKenzie from Deirdre. I purposely took a few steps away from Alan and Barry, putting some distance between my child and the murderer.

"Who the heck are these two?" Alan asked.

I was about to say that they were my partners-in-crime, but I realized it was a bad idea to phrase it that way, since we technically *had* committed a crime. "They're my assistants. They helped me get into the building."

"Uh, more like *you're* the assistant, I'm the mastermind," Deirdre said.

"What does that make me?" Mel asked.

"A bunch of lucky idiots," Alan said. "I can't *believe* I got caught by a group of wannabe detectives."

"That's not very nice," Mel scolded him.

"Yeah, well, what do you *expect* me to say?" Alan asked. "Am I supposed to be *happy* that you caught me? I'm going to go to jail for murder for the rest of my life!"

"Are you confessing to the murder of Mr. O'Neill?" Barry asked.

Alan sighed. "There's no point in denying it any longer. Yes, I killed Mr. O'Neill. I thought he was going to fire me, so I decided to fire *him*...permanently."

Barry forced Alan to sit down and cuffed him to the chair, so he couldn't escape. I felt a lot safer with two pairs of handcuffs on the culprit. Barry refused to let any of us leave, until the police arrived. I tried telling Deirdre and Mel what happened, but Alan interrupted several times, saying I was a fool who didn't know anything. Eventually, I decided to stop talking.

It took about forty minutes for Detective Dodd to arrive, since he wasn't on duty at the time. My wife Brittany showed up before him. Needless to say, she wasn't happy.

"I give you the night off, and not only do you go running around downtown with two other women, you get yourself *arrested?*" she asked.

"Yeah, he's kind of an idiot," Deirdre said.

"Shut up, Deirdre," Brittany said.

"For the record, I would like to say that this is 100% Deirdre's fault, not mine," I said. "It was her idea to break into my old office and look for clues."

"Oh my God, Deirdre, Ned dumped you in *high school*," Brittany said. "Get over it already! Stop trying to ruin his life!"

"How pathetic do you think I am?" Deirdre said. "I have better things to worry about than your diaper daddy of a husband."

"And *you*, Mel," Brittany said. "You...why are you dressed like you're about to win an awards show?"

"I figured if I was going to get arrested, I might as well do it in style," Mel shrugged.

"I like your outfit," Barry said, smiling at her.

"Don't get any ideas, Barry," I said. "She's married with a kid."

Barry stopped smiling. "You used her to distract me? That's cold, man. I thought we were buddies."

"Desperate times call for desperate measures," I shrugged.

"*Desperate* is right," Brittany said. "You'll be sleeping on the couch for a month after this."

"Good," I said. "I'm tired of sleeping in the bed with you and the baby. She kicks."

"Wait, which one kicks?" Alan asked. "The wife or the baby?"

Brittany glared at him. "I take it this is the Alan you've told me so much about."

"Oh, that's him," I said, giving Alan my best Angry Dad Look, "and he just tried to frame me for murder, multiple times."

"I can see why you don't like him," Brittany said.

Detective Dodd showed up about five minutes after Brittany did. I figured he would let me tell what happened in front of everyone else. You know, give me a chance to explain my great detective skills! That's what happens in *Harvey Brothers* books, but it turns out that in real life the police don't like getting lectured about how to do their jobs by amateur detectives. Who knew?

It only took three sentences before Dodd interrupted my monologue. And once the precedent of "it's okay to interrupt Ned" was set, there was no stopping it. I was interrupted by Dodd, Alan, Deirdre—*especially* Deirdre—and occasionally Brittany. I came off looking less like a hero, and more like an idiot who had stumbled upon the mystery solution by accident. Yes, it was a coincidence that I broke into the crime scene shortly before the culprit did, but I was fairly confident I would have solved the mystery on my own, if Alan hadn't interrupted me.

I tried to direct the topic of conversation to the amazing way I had handled myself during the culprit confrontation, but everyone was more interested in hearing the details of Alan's crime. I suppose that was for the best. It would have been too much of a distraction if I had Alan repeat his rant about how much he hates living with a stay-at-home parent.

Alan was still angry, but he seemed to know that the jig was up. He readily confessed to everything, multiple times.

Dodd seemed more than happy with the situation, and he had another officer take Alan away in a police car. "I'll let the higher-ups decide what to do next," he said. "I doubt they'll need your statements—not when Mr. Stacker has admitted his guilt—but just in case, I'll get your contact information. After that..."

"We'll be free to go?" Deirdre asked.

"I *should* put you in holding for interfering with an active police investigation," Dodd said, "but I suppose I owe you some gratitude for solving the case."

"Thanks!" I said. "After all, if it wasn't for us, the results of your murder investigation would have been...*dead wrong!*"

Detective Dodd pulled out his handcuffs and slapped them on my wrists. "Changed my mind. You're coming downtown."

"Oh come on!" I complained.

"So your first week as a stay-at-home dad, and you get arrested," Brittany said. "You are setting *such* a bad example for McKenzie."

"I could have told you that marrying him was a bad idea," Deirdre said.

Dodd read me my rights and let me sweat for a while, before removing the handcuffs and letting me go. "I can't arrest you for real, unless the company decides to press charges," he said, "but I hope you've learned your lesson about breaking and entering into locked buildings."

"Yes, sir," I said meekly.

Brittany drove me and McKenzie back home, after that. She gave me a stern lecture on how disappointed she was in me, but she only got halfway through before she burst out laughing. She said she was so proud of me for proving my innocence, and to also never do that again, or else she really *would* make me sleep on the couch.

I promised her that the next time I did a secret murder investigation, she would be invited. Brittany seemed happy with that, and she made me retell the entire story at least three times on the way home.

Deirdre was the exact opposite. Once we were outside the building, she said I was a stupid idiot who almost got her arrested, and she never wanted to see me again. It was surprisingly similar to the lecture she had given me when we broke up back in high school. I talked it over with Brittany, and we decided that apologizing to her would be the right thing to do.

So at Friday's meeting of the Mystery Club, I showed up with a surprise cake for her. I baked it myself, and I wrote "Detective Deirdre" on top. At least, I *tried* to. The letters got smudged, so I turned the decoration into a magnifying glass, halfway through. Deirdre had three pieces and knuckled me on the arm afterwards, saying I wasn't bad for a Harvey Brothers fan. I think that means she doesn't hate me anymore.

Together, we told the other Mystery Club members about our little escapade. While I admit that Deirdre's "pretending to be a radio" trick had been clever enough to fool Natalie, I think it was exaggerating to say she was the hero, and I was her dumb sidekick who almost ruined everything. Good thing I was there to set the record straight.

The other club members seemed entertained by our story. Sherlock Holmes said we did a good job, Fake Frenchman said we were lucky Alan didn't have a weapon with him when he confronted me, and Kay said I should have body-slammed Alan the instant he showed up in Mr. O'Neill's office.

There was another positive development with Deirdre. I think she took it to heart when I told her Scott has a crush on her. Scott says Deirdre been visiting his pizza store a lot more often now, and he swears that he's going to ask her out soon. I'll believe it when I see it.

Barry was angry with me over what happened. He seems to think that I made him look incompetent by sneaking in the building without his notice, *and* capturing a criminal without his help. I sent him an apology letter, but I never got a response. Now that I'm not working in the office anymore, I'll probably never see him again.

I never saw Natalie again, either. College students and stay-at-home parents don't really occupy the same social circles, you know? I hope she did well in her classes, and she graduated college without a huge amount of student debt. Of course, my college degree wasn't being used for anything now that I was watching McKenzie all the time, so what do I know?

The only person from my work who contacted me was Kelly. She sent me an outstanding employee recognition award, along with a note saying that the award usually came with a small bonus, but she had taken it away because I broke over a dozen company rules. Also, my ID card access had been revoked, so if I tried breaking into the building again, I would be arrested for real. I sent her a text message, saying thanks.

I wasn't quite sure what to expect from the next meeting of the baby playtime group. After all, I knew Alan's wife Roberta would be there.

She pulled me aside before the start of the meeting and apologized to me, on Alan's behalf. I tried to brush it off, because she honestly had nothing to apologize for, but she had insisted. Later on after the playtime group started, she said this would be her last time attending. A family emergency had come up, she said, and her parents would be taking care of the baby while she looked for work. I never saw her or Alan again after that. I hoped everything worked out okay for her.

Mel didn't hold any grudges against me for almost getting her in trouble with the law. She seemed to think that the entire night had been a great joke, and she insisted on calling me her spy buddy for the next few weeks. She gave me some free tips as to how I could improve my wardrobe, but when I saw how expensive some of her outfits were, I said thanks, but no thanks. I would need a full-time job, just for those clothes.

As for the other moms, none of them had any idea what had happened at my old job. I made sure it stayed that way. How would you even begin a conversation like that, anyway?

"Hi, I like your daughter, and by the way, did you know I was framed for murder last week? I broke into the office and almost got arrested, but that's okay. The culprit was Roberta's husband. Isn't that just like a soap opera?"

Detective Dodd called me a few days later as part of a follow-up before he officially closed the books on the case. I think he just wanted to make sure I was okay after my near brush with death. I told him not to worry, but he still insisted on giving me the contact information of a psychiatrist he knows, just in case I had any problems. I thanked him for his concern.

"We've finished going over the diaper bag you left at the crime scene," he said. "It's been cleared. You can take it home with you, now."

"Oh, thank goodness," I said. "I've been using an old backpack as a diaper bag this past weekend, and people keep asking me if I'm going camping."

"Did anyone actually *say* that, or did they just tell you to take a hike?"

"That's not a bad joke," I said. "You're getting better at this, Detective Dodd."

He grunted in response.

We always keep a change of clothes for McKenzie inside the diaper bag, in case she ever needs to switch clothes while we were on the go. It wasn't until a few weeks later that she spit up all over herself, while we were at the grocery store. I changed her outfit in the bathroom, and when I got home, I decided to clean out the diaper bag for real. That thing was a mess of toys, diapers and burp cloths.

To my surprise, I found several of Mr. O'Neill's lottery tickets buried inside. They must have fallen into my bag, when I bumped the drawer of his desk. I guess the police thought they weren't important enough to remove them from the diaper bag.

I paused, as I looked at them. Alan had seen the boss with a pink piece of paper that would "solve all the company's financial problems". If it wasn't a pink slip, what was it? O'Neill only had one other type of pink paper: the drawer full of lottery tickets.

Was it possible? Could Mr. O'Neill have won the lottery? But if he had, why did he come into work and act like everything was normal? Not to mention he would have kept such a valuable ticket on his person, not in a desk drawer with several other discarded tickets. And of course, lottery games are based on chance, and should not be played for investment purposes. Still...

Just to make sure, I got on my computer and looked up the winning lottery numbers for the day of the murder. Most of the tickets were worthless, but one of them had five matching numbers. It didn't have all six numbers, so it didn't get the big jackpot, but five was definitely enough to qualify for a prize.

My eyes went wide when I saw just how much the prize was.

"This ticket is worth $60,000!" I exclaimed. "We're rich, McKenzie! We could buy a new house with that kind of money! ...Well, maybe not, but we *can* afford to send you to daycare while I go back to work. What do you think of that?"

I looked down at McKenzie, who was lying in my lap. She smiled at me, raised her hand up towards my face and said, "Aaa."

I smiled back. "You're right. We can put this money in your college fund instead. Daddy doesn't need to go back to work. He wants to stay right here with you."

# The End

# Ned's Favorite Stay-At-Home Recipes

*Boxed Food*

Ingredients required:

Box of food

Step 1: Buy food in a box.
Step 2: Follow the instructions on the box.
Step 3: Enjoy!


*Apples with Applesauce*

Ingredients required:

Apples
Applesauce

Step 1. Cut apple into slices.
Step 2. Put apple slices in applesauce.
Step 3. Enjoy!


*Baby's Mashed Potatoes*

Ingredients required:

Baby
Potato

Step 1. Put potato in a pot of water. Heat until it boils.
Step 2. Remove potato. It's hot, so let it cool on a towel or something for ten minutes.
Step 3. Put potato in front of baby. Baby will mash it for you. Enjoy your mashed potatoes!
Step 4: Clean up afterwards. (*Note: not recommended for beginners*)

*Exploding Broccoli*

Ingredients required:

Broccoli

Step 1. Put broccoli in microwave until it explodes.
Step 2. Throw out broccoli.
Step 3. Order pizza instead.


*Deirdre's Surprise Cake*

Ingredients required:

Frosting

Step 1. Buy a blank cake from a store.
Step 2. Write a message on top with frosting.
Step 3. Pretend you made it yourself.


*Chicken Tikka Masala Burritos*

Ingredients required:

Beef
Tortillas
Chicken Tikka Masala

Step 1. Brown beef and drain.
Step 2. Add bottle of chicken tikka masala. Cook on medium high heat for five minutes, so the sauce is warm and settles into the meat. You should probably stir it or something, too.
Step 3. Hope your wife doesn't notice you used chicken stuff on beef. Mine did, but maybe yours isn't as observant.
Step 4. Wrap meat mixture in tortilla. Serve with other burrito toppings, if desired.

*Easy Three-Step Lasagna*

Ingredients required:

1 pound ground beef
1/2 pound sausage
16 ounce can tomatoes
6 ounce can tomato paste
1 garlic clove, crushed
1/2 teaspoon salt
1/4 teaspoon pepper
8 ounces ricotta
1 egg
1/4 cup parmesan
1/2 teaspoon oregano
1/4 teaspoon basil
1 tablespoon parsley
6-9 lasagna noodles
2 cups mozzarella

Step 1. Cook beef and sausage together on the stove until browned. Drain. Stir in tomatoes, tomato paste, garlic, salt and pepper. Alternately, use a can of spaghetti sauce in place of the tomatoes and spices. In a separate bowl, mix ricotta, egg, parmesan, oregano, basil and parsley. Alternately, you could use a carton of cottage cheese for the cheese mixture. In a slow cooker, do a layer of noodles, a layer of meat, a layer of cheese, and a layer of mozzarella. Then, repeat those four layers: noodles, meat, cheese and mozzarella. Most recipes say to repeat the layers three times, but I don't have any containers that are tall enough to hold three layers of lasagna, so I only do two. Cook for five to six hours on low heat. Cut the lasagna into pieces.
Step 2. Serve the lasagna.
Step 3. Enjoy!

## Harvey Brothers Mini-Mystery: The Secret of Lilac Inn

I showed this book to my wife, and she said that it was completely unnecessary for me to include the part where I sing a song about tummy time. "You don't have to put the story on hold, in order to share your musical talents. Besides, it's a book. Nobody can hear you sing."

I responded with a joke about audiobooks, but her comment reminded me of the fourth Harvey Brothers book, <u>The Secret of Lilac Inn</u>. Chapter 12 of that book is *completely* out of place. The Harvey Brothers are in the middle of solving a kidnapping mystery, when they stop to find a lost dog instead.

As it turns out, the only reason they included that chapter is because the original manuscript was one chapter too short. The publisher threatened not to pay the author, if they didn't write an extra four pages. And so, a ridiculous filler chapter was born.

I thought I would include this filler chapter in my book, for the sake of historical interest. Also, my manuscript is one chapter short.

\* \* \*

Fred and Jim Harvey looked at each other and nodded, knowing what they had to do. They had to break down the door to the gardener's shed and steal the map before the culprits returned.

"Let's both kick on three," Fred said, holding up three fingers. "Three. Two. O—"

"*Jim! I've been looking all over for you!*" a voice called.

The Harveys stopped and turned around. Waving at them from the street was Iolanthe Merton, Jim's good friend. They sometimes dated each other, but their relationship never got too serious, because Jim had no idea how to pronounce her name.

The Harveys quickly jogged over to Iolanthe, before they could be spotted. "Jeepers, Iolanthe, what brings you here?" Fred asked.

"You like solving mysteries, right?" Iolanthe asked, smiling brightly. "I've got a great one for you!"

"Gee, we're kind of in the middle of something here," Jim said.

"I don't care!" Iolanthe barked. "This is important! I lost my dog, and I can't find him anywhere!"

Fred looked skeptical, but Jim didn't want to upset his sometimes-girlfriend. "Sure, we can help you find him," Jim said quickly, before Fred could tell Iolanthe to leave them alone. "Where did you last see him?"

"Fido was in my bedroom, and the door has been locked this whole time! That's what makes this so mysterious!" Iolanthe pouted for a few seconds, then fluffed her long, brown hair. "You *will* find him, won't you, Jim?"

"I wouldn't dream of doing anything else," Jim said.

"I'd rather go eat a sandwich," Fred muttered.

"What was that?" Iolanthe asked.

"I said I can't wait to get started!" Fred said.

The three teenagers piled into the Harveys' yellow car. Fred drove to the Merton house, while Jim and Iolanthe shared the backseat together.

"What were you two doing at Lilac Inn anyway?" Iolanthe asked.

"We think the owner of the inn is secretly an imposter, who's trying to cover for a gang of thieves," Fred said seriously.

"You mean the thieves who robbed poor Mrs. McGillacuddy's house last week? When I heard that she lost her wedding ring, I was so sad, I sat down and cried for an hour," Iolanthe said. "It sure is swell of you two boys to try to help recover the stolen goods. But what makes you think the thieves are at the inn?"

"The thieves have to be staying somewhere around here," Jim said. "And when we asked the inn owner if he had any suspicious guests recently, he yelled at us!"

"And?" Iolanthe asked.

"And what?" Jim asked. "That's all that happened."

"You can't accuse someone of harboring criminals, just because they yelled at you," Iolanthe said.

"That's not all," Fred said. "When we asked him about the baseball game two Fridays ago, he said it was great fun. But when the Yellow Socks played two weeks ago, it wasn't on a Friday! *It was on a Thursday!*"

Jim nodded. "That's why we figure he's an imposter."

"Maybe he just got the date wrong," Iolanthe said.

"Do you really think someone could forget a date that's only two weeks out?" Jim asked.

"Yes," Iolanthe said. "Remember last month, when you missed our movie date?"

Jim groaned. That particular event had been a major sore spot in their relationship. "It wasn't on purpose!" He defended himself. "I told you, Fred and I were kidnapped by smugglers who were hiding drugs inside of golf balls. They tied us up on a boat and sent us out to sea, where a shark bit the ropes—"

"That's no excuse! You should have been at home, preparing for our night out!" Iolanthe said. "I had to beg my father for weeks to let me go, and when he finally agreed, I had no date! He'll probably never let me go out again!"

"Fred, please help me explain what happened to her," Jim begged.

Fred sighed. "For the last time, I'm not getting involved in your argument. I won't pick sides between you two. Although if I had the choice, I would much rather go to the movies than tangle with sharks."

Iolanthe smiled at Fred, and Jim felt a pang of jealousy. And yet, this unwanted emotion was not enough to stimulate his dull mind and cause him to realize that he should be more considerate of his special friend.

They soon arrived at the Merton house. The fair Iolanthe led them to her bedroom, and Jim couldn't help but gulp nervously in anticipation. He had never seen the inside of a woman's bedroom before, much less Iolanthe's. What would his parents say if they found out?

Iolanthe seemed to be thinking along the same lines. "If my father asks what you were doing here today..."

"We should leave the door open, just in case," Fred said reasonably.

"No!" Jim said. "I mean, we can't risk contaminating the crime scene like that."

Fred shot his brother a skeptical look, as he opened the door. The Harveys were surprised to find that Iolanthe's bedroom was a perfectly normal bedroom, just like theirs. The only main differences were the fact that Iolanthe's room was meant for one person, and she had an extra mirror where the Harveys had a sports banner.

"You search the room, I'll check the exits," Fred said to his brother.

"But there aren't any exits," Iolanthe said. "The only way Fido could have left is through the door, and I already told you it was locked the whole time."

"And you're sure he was inside the room when you locked the door?" Jim asked.

"Positive," Iolanthe said. "I always lock the door when I leave my room."

Jim examined the bed, while Fred examined the window. "The blankets have been disturbed," Jim announced. "This bed has *definitely* been used recently."

"I use my bed every night," Iolanthe said.

"No, I mean Fido jumped on the bed," Jim said.

"But could Fido have jumped from the bed to the window?" Fred wondered aloud. "The window appears to be undisturbed, and I doubt Fido has the ability to shut the window behind him."

"The window by the dresser is open," Jim said. "But it's too high for our spunky pup to reach."

"He could have climbed up the individual dresser drawers, like a staircase," Fred said. "If they were open, that is."

"I'll check," Jim said. He pulled open the top drawer with a forceful tug.

"Jim, no!" Iolanthe cried.

Jim was surprised when the drawer flew out of the dresser, but the *true* surprise was the drawer's contents. It contained all of Iolanthe's frilliest undergarments! Terrified, Jim screamed and fell backwards, bashing into Iolanthe's bed. He fell to the ground, clutching his leg. A loud bark was heard, and the missing dog appeared.

"Fido!" Iolanthe said.

"He was under the bed the whole time!" Fred said.

Fido jumped playfully, and the two teens laughed at the happy resolution to the problem. The cheerful moment was soon swept away, when Mr. Merton appeared.

"What is going on here?" Mr. Merton asked ferociously. His furious eyes swept the room and landed upon Jim, who was still lying on the floor, covered with Iolanthe's undergarments.

"*Jim Harvey!*" Mr. Merton shouted. "What are you doing in my daughter's room, with her clothing?"

Jim tried to explain, but he stumbled over his words and soon discovered that Iolanthe's father was as hard to convince as Iolanthe was. Three minutes later, Jim was violently thrown out of the Merton house and ordered never to return. Fred and Iolanthe would have stepped in to defend Jim's honor, but they were too busy laughing.

"I should probably get going," Fred said. "Jim's going to be awfully sore about this."

"He'll get over it," Iolanthe said. "Good luck catching the thieves! If you can get them as easily as you found Fido, they'll be in jail by the end of the week!"

Fred thanked Iolanthe and left the house. An embarrassed Jim was waiting for him in the car.

166

"So, you really like—" Fred began to say.

"I don't want to talk about it," Jim muttered.

And so the Harveys returned to the Lilac Inn, and they stopped outside the gardener's shed. It was the exact same spot they were in, at the start of the chapter. To the unobservant reader, it was as if nothing had happened at all.

## About the Author

Michael Gray is a stay-at-home dad who has not solved any murder mysteries in real life, unfortunately. His YouTube channel, Arglefumph, has amassed over 58 million views. He is the #1 online reviewer for many mystery book series, including *Hardy Boys Casefiles, Nancy Drew Files, Nancy Drew / Hardy Boys Supermystery, Nancy Drew Girl Detective, Boxcar Children* and *Encyclopedia Brown*. In some cases, he's the *only* person who has done video reviews for those series.

He has written a number of videogames, including *Cat President, The Courting of Miss Bennet: A Pride and Prejudice Game* and *The Pizza Delivery Boy Who Saved the World*. This is his first novel. He lives in Oregon with his wife and two children.

Pictured: Michael and his infant daughter Rosie,
who provided much of the inspiration for this book.

# Acknowledgements

Special thanks to Katherine Bacher, for her editorial assistance

Special thanks to Half-Moon Media, for designing the cover

Special thanks to Bridgitte Waldrop, for introducing me to cozy mysteries

Made in the USA
Middletown, DE
09 May 2020